Bog Men

Joyce Keller Walsh

PublishAmerica
Baltimore

© 2007 by Joyce Keller Walsh.
All rights reserved. No part of this book may be reproduced, stored in a retrieval system or transmitted in any form or by any means without the prior written permission of the publishers, except by a reviewer who may quote brief passages in a review to be printed in a newspaper, magazine or journal.

First printing

All characters in this book are fictitious, and any resemblance to real persons, living or dead, is coincidental.

PublishAmerica has allowed this work to remain exactly as the author intended, verbatim, without editorial input.

ISBN: 1-60441-317-4
PUBLISHED BY PUBLISHAMERICA, LLLP
www.publishamerica.com
Baltimore

Printed in the United States of America

For John, Always

With Special Thanks to:
Joyce Griffin and *Joan Myers Horton*
for Friendship and Support

Illustrated map: Sarah Bender Pasternak

Cover art: Daniel Cooney
dcooney59@yahoo.com

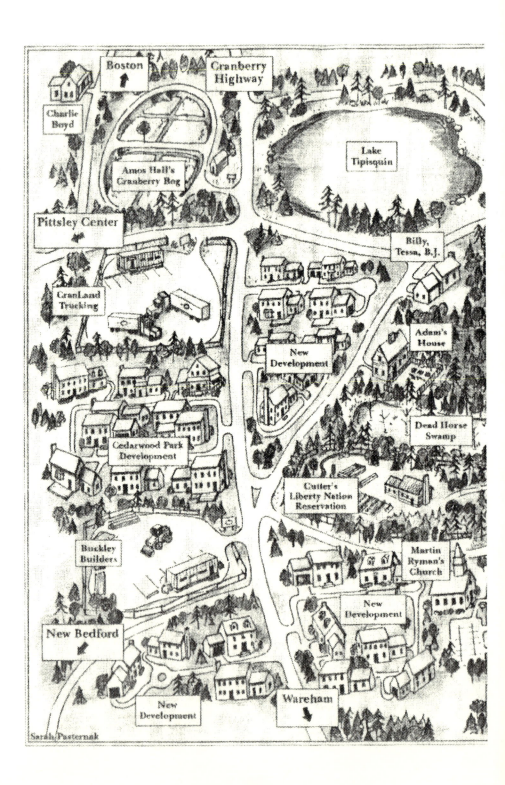

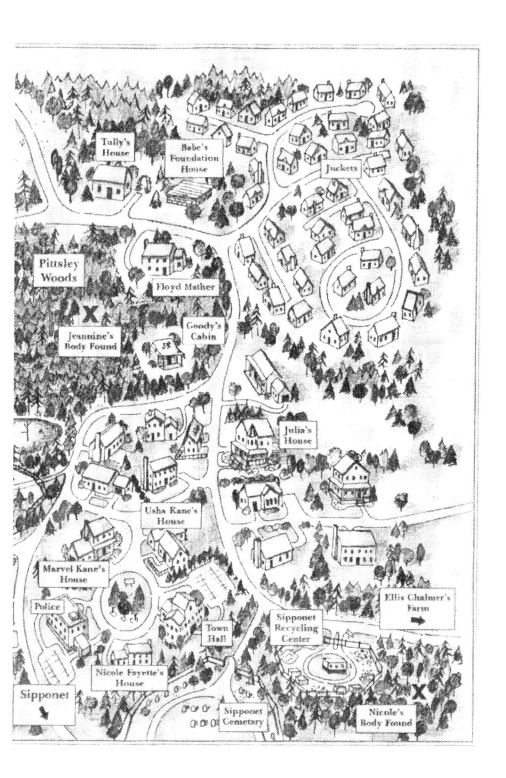

Bog Men

Prologue

It was a peculiar day, this out-of-place October day. Not an Indian Summer day because there had been no hard frost yet, but not a typical autumn day. It was a day to admit the vagaries of nature, a day of contrasts and transitions, a day to tantalize and disappoint. It was a hot day to work all day in the sun.

Focused on separating weeds from cranberry vines, B.J. Jensen paid little attention to the small Cambodian woman next to him until she straightened up, arched her back, and took a deep breath of the moist stagnant air. When he first met Mrs. Nim, with her flowing black pants and meager white blouse, he thought she might have been more at home in a rice paddy than a Massachusetts cranberry bog.

As he worked, the only sounds he was aware of came from the variable buzz of insects loud and soft, the distant honking of migrating geese in a straggly formation, and the hand-rustle of weeders pulling up invasive plants. There were no clouds in the cobalt-blue sky. No breezes swaying the pine needles or rippling through the leaves whose names the woman next to him would not know, the colors of which she had never seen before: oaks that were red and brown like potato skins, Golden Birch, scarlet Red Maples, orange Sugar Maples, and Black Maple leaves as yellow as butterfly wings. She would not yet know, as he did, their portent of a New England winter only weeks away.

"You see Ponlok?" Chaya Nim asked, turning towards him, her brow furrowed.

B.J. stood upright and stretched his sore muscles. From under his Red Sox cap, he glanced around the dirt ring-road and beyond into the thick circle of woods. There was no sign of her son.

B.J. and Ponlok were the only teenagers working the Hall bog this season. Except for himself, all of the weeders were Cambodian, bussed up in the morning the fifteen or so miles from Fall River then back at the end of the day. The two boys had started together in May and spent every Sunday pulling out blue and white asters, fern, and Joe Pye Weed (sometimes called Queen of the Meadow) which B.J. used to pick for his mother when he was little. She had loved the long slender leaves and the sweetly fragrant lavender clusters of blossoms. The purpley-blue asters that he pulled out here were the same as those she used to keep in jelly-jar vases on the windowsill over the sink. Who decided what was a flower and what was a weed? Here, it was clear enough, but there was a host of unwanted plants he was tearing out of the bog that in other places would be a welcome addition to a wildflower garden—except, of course, poison ivy, maple sprigs, and assorted mongrel weeds that choked the cranberry vines and would strangle any less aggressive plant. Bogging, he supposed, was just perennial gardening on a larger scale.

This Hall bog was only a twenty-acre family bog, one of many that Amos Hall owned. But this was his oldest and not dependent on pesticides for weed control. This would be the last weeding of the season before the bogs were harvested. Even with a late start this year due to a cold wet spring, it would all be over by the end of the month.

"Where Ponlok?" she repeated insistently.

A wide straw hat shadowed her pinched face as she squinted across the bent backs of the other workers. She was very frail, B.J. thought, so frail and wispy that a monsoon wind might have swirled her up from that faraway country and swept her across the ocean only to let her float down here like one of the falling leaves.

He pointed to the far end of the bog. "He's probably gone into the woods."

Chaya Nim looked in the direction of his finger, then shook her head at him uncomprehendingly.

He mimed zipping his fly up and down. Briefly he wondered if she knew about zippers and flys, but Mrs. Nim nodded and bent back to her weeding.

Although B.J. was younger than most of the Cambodians, Amos had put him in charge not only because he lived here in Pittsley, but most likely because Amos could tell him in English what he wanted the weeders to do. Nonetheless, he proudly told his father he'd been made crew chief and his dad was pleased. He felt the burden of pleasing his father even more now that his mother was dead.

B.J. glanced at his watch with the steel bracelet, a birthday present from his parents along with a Swiss Army Knife he prized but never used. Some of his friends had received cars on their sixteenth birthday, but that was far beyond what his parents could afford and he didn't allow himself to yearn for one. At least not seriously.

Thank God it was nearly time to quit. He knew now why none of the locals wanted to weed the bogs anymore: it was sweaty, miserable work and one thing for sure, no bog owner was going to lose his profits because the workers ate his crop. Raw cranberries made your mouth pucker just thinking about them. He wiped the sweat from his face with the bottom of his t-shirt and went back to work.

He really liked Lucky even though the boy was two years younger than himself. Lucky was small but strong. And smart. And he had a sense of playfulness that appealed to B.J. He wondered if Lucky had to wear those black coolie pants and white blouse-shirt to school in Fall River. He hoped not. He could just hear the other kids calling him 'girlie-man' or worse. What Lucky needed was a pair of jeans, a sweatshirt, and motorcycle boots instead of those froggy green flip-flops. He knew his new friend well enough now that maybe he could offer Lucky some of his outgrown clothes.

As he yanked up the weeds by the roots and stuffed them into an industrial-weight black plastic bag, B.J. listened to a Carolina wren who had flown by and perched somewhere above in the treetop. It was probably an unmated male—like himself, he thought wryly. Most of the songbirds were gone now, but these little chestnut birds with the cream-colored breasts had become permanent residents in New England right through the winter. He always paid careful attention to birdsongs and tired to identify the notes. This was a melody he could almost visualize. Di-doodela-doodela-doodela. Did the bird know his song instinctively or did he have to learn it? Maybe a little of both—also like himself. He loved music. It made him feel...how could he describe it...abstract. When he played the violin, he wasn't William Jensen, Jr. He wasn't almost seventeen. He didn't think about his mother being dead or about school or work or Ruth Washburn who barely acknowledged him, or the red-and-white vintage Corvette he saw in the school parking lot. He was—

B.J. suddenly felt a light tug at his waistband.

Mrs. Nim shook her head at him anxiously.

"No Ponlok."

He stood up again, looming over her, flexing his shoulders and pulling his wet shirt away from his chest. Sweat saturated his hair, dripped off his nose, and trickled down his neck and back. He scanned the circumference of the bog, swatting away insects from his eyes and mouth. But Lucky wasn't there and he should have been back by now.

"Has anybody seen Lucky?" he shouted to the others.

There was no reply.

Lucky's mother then called out something that B.J. couldn't understand, and one by one the Cambodians shook their heads.

Sunday, October 1st

"Eminent domain, my hairy ass—"

Cutter Briggs stood scratching his croakies and his voice rose an octave as he said what they were all thinking. His long hair and chin-beard were dyed black now to cover the streaks of grey, something his new wife Angel had prompted. But none of his friends would mention the fact that his beard was growing out white at the roots

"—it's tyranny is what it is. *Tyranny*!"

The five friends—Cutter Briggs, Billy Jensen, Elmer Goodson, Arlo Tulliver, and Adam Sabeski—were gathered in Adam's livingroom for their ritual Sunday dinner. Mindful of old Goody's diabetes, Adam made baked cod and stewed tomatoes this week, along with a crockpot of kale soup. The kale, potatoes, carrots, onions, and tomatoes had come from his back garden. Tully brought the last of his summer squash, Billy provided a loaf of crusty French bread that he'd baked himself, and Cutter supplied the moonshine labeled 'Liberty Juice' from his own stills. Goody usually brought something old—an odd machine part or a strange antique tool that had some lost purpose—that they could all ponder about. Today, however, the unidentified tool lay on the floor without discussion.

"*You* got nothing to worry about," Tully said, his weathered face showing disgust in his downturned mouth. "Not since you become an Indian."

"I didn't become an Indian." Cutter's aquamarine eyes blazed. "I'm as Swamp Yankee as anybody. But there's Wampanoag blood in the Briggs line and I got the benefit of it."

It wasn't so long ago that Cutter had emancipated himself from the town of Pittlsey, the Commonwealth of Massachusetts, and the United States of America. Cutter and his brothers and sympathizers had formed Liberty Nation, their own self-sufficient commune. Initially, it was to be a secession, but since that was unlikely to work Adam had managed to finesse a connection between Cutter and the Wampanoags. Now Liberty Nation was a recognized Reservation and Cutter legally thumbed his nose at the Government.

"Well, they can't take your land by eminent domain is what I mean." Tully set down his plate of food on the large wooden-spool table in the center of the five overstuffed armchairs. He dropped his callused hands into his lap. "I bought that land and built my house with my own sweat. I been living there for almost fifty years and now what am I going to do? I got nowhere else to go. Where are we supposed to go, Doris and me?"

With each of the men contemplating Tully's question, the room fell silent. There was no ticking of a wall clock; no television, DVD, or CD player. It was a livingroom that hadn't seen much change in the twenty years Adam owned it, nor in the nearly one hundred years since the house had been built. Even though Julia, Adam's ladyfriend…he still didn't know what else to call her…had used all her psychology to try to convince him to upgrade the room, to replace the spool-table with a real coffetable, and the old ragged chairs with new ones, she had ultimately conceded defeat. And although Adam finally agreed to non-frilly curtains, the floors were still bare, the walls still barnboard, and the overall effect still ramshackle and utterly masculine. The potbellied stove still stood in the middle of the room, unused for the summer months, and the bookshelves in the corner behind the oak desk were still filled with a combination of veterinary books, animal skulls, and bottles of moonshine.

In truth, Julia's regular presence had made very little impact on the old rustic livingroom. Right now, she was in California visiting her daughter, son-in-law, and first grandchild after attending some psychology conference. For the two weeks she'd been gone, Adam had custody of

Catastrophe, her Golden Retriever who currently lay at his feet sleeping with intermittent snores and paw-wiggling. *What is she dreaming?* he wondered. Cat, now grey-muzzled and overweight, probably hadn't chased anything in years. Puppy dreams, maybe.

Inexorably, his thoughts reverted to his work. Not only was he the town veterinarian, he investigated all the animal cruelty cases. Over the past few weeks he'd been preoccupied with reports—the most recent one, yesterday—of rustlers. "Rustlers" the farmers told him, as though they were cattle barons on the open range and he was the Sheriff. But he would hardly call it 'rustling' just because a few cows and goats were gone. Actually, one per week. Expensive ones. Belted Galway calves. Saanen kids.

He'd reported it as felony theft to the Chief of Police, Carson Burke, but there wasn't a high priority on a few missing farm animals compared with drugs, housebreaks, drunk driving, assaults, and other crimes that crossed his desk. Truth to tell, there wasn't very much crime in Pittsley— but there wasn't much of a police force either, only three full-time officers besides himself and three shift-dispatchers.

Somebody was probably selling black-market beef and goat meat, Burke suggested. But Adam was unconvinced. Who would rustle a prize Saanen for goat meat? And there weren't any predators around that could take down a cow or goat. The coyotes went primarily for small prey even though they might occasionally take a deer.

"Do you have the letter with you, Tully?" Billy asked, breaking the oppressive silence in the room and jogging Adam back to the subject at hand.

Tully reached into his pants pocket. He never wore any trousers other old green farmer's chinos or an even older pair of baker's pants, black and white checked with the cuffs cut off. His second-hand workshirts varied from blue to green with someone else's name printed on the breast pocket. Bob, of Wareham Auto Supply. Mike, of Acushnet Towing. There was one that said Burt, and Cutter had seized the opportunity, as he usually did, to bait Tully.

"What's that say, 'Bev'?"

"Burt," Tully growled. "Can't you read? *Burt.*"

"Looks like Bev."
"It ain't Bev, it's Burt."
"Burt, your name?"
"Don't matter what it says, it's my shirt."
"Okay, Bev."

Tully hadn't talked to Cutter for several days after that one. Cutter of course had not been daunted. He did it again the following week on another topic just as he had for countless weeks in the past and would continue to do for countless weeks to come.

Tully passed the folded envelope to Adam. It was printed with the seal of the town and the return address of the town counsel.

"Read it out loud," Goody grumbled, "so Billy can hear it."

Goody was being only half-considerate. Billy may have been blind, but Goody was getting cataracts and would not admit it. Adam had driven him to take the peep-and-squint test and now the ophthalmologist wanted to schedule surgery. Adam knew his old friend would never consider it if it weren't for the consequences. Goody couldn't continue to live alone in his shack in the woods and be independent if his vision were impaired. "A man's gotta see his enemies coming," Goody said to the eye doctor, who blanched.

As Adam read the letter aloud, Tully sat with his head bowed. He ran his thick fingers over his scalp. What there was left of his hair was in short grey bristles. Doris had used the electric Oster to shear her husband's head again.

When he finished reading, Adam said, "But they still have to go through due process. It doesn't mean they'll be able to do it. There'll have to be hearings—"

"Crapola," Goody interrupted between mouthfuls of fresh baked cod. "What government wants, government gets."

"Not always." Cutter sat back down opposite Goody with a Cheshire cat grin.

"I don't understand," Billy said, staring unseeing at the ceiling and using his left index finger to guide the fish onto his fork. "That happens in third-world countries with revolutions and dictators. How can the State do this? I thought they could only take your land for back taxes or if there was some kind of public works project."

"I pay my taxes," Tully said as though accused. "I go right down to the Town Hall and pay them the day after I get the bill. I give the cash right to the Treasurer. I got all my receipts."

"We know that," Billy said. "I just meant that things like this aren't supposed to happen here."

"That's what they thought in New London and a bunch of other places," Cutter retorted, "until all them people lost their homes so some developers could build a mall and an office building and a yuppie gym or something. The city just handed over the land because they could get more revenue from businesses than from the homeowners. And the Supreme Court upheld it. Shit, that's what we've come to."

Cat decided to stand up, circle around three times and fling herself back onto the floor to stretch out. Adam absently bent over to pat the dog at his feet.

"I wonder," he said to Tully, "if yours is the only land they're confiscating."

Tully scowled. "I don't care about nobody else. I'm not leaving my house."

"Maybe you should get a lawyer," Billy suggested.

"Screw lawyers," Cutter said, "'cause all they do is screw you."

"But he needs legal advice," Billy said.

"What he needs," Goody replied definitively, "is a shotgun."

In the quiet of agreement, Adam heard someone approach the front door.

"That's B.J.," Billy said, always the first to identify a sound even as Cat cocked her broad golden head then put it back down. He knew his son's footsteps as surely as he knew his voice. "But he usually goes right home after working the bog."

"Come on in, B.J." Adam shouted at the first knock.

The boy entered with a harried expression that captured their immediate attention. B.J. quickly explained what had transpired, that no one could find Ponlok, and should they call the police?

Adam immediately phoned Chief Burke.

* * *

Three thousand miles away, Julia sat in her daughter's kitchen holding her infant grandson. Jesse grabbed onto her finger with his chubby little hands and burbled. She cooed back to him in perfect communication. She blew little kisses on his toes and the baby laughed and kicked his bare feet in delight.

Her son-in-law Paul was washing the dishes in the double sink as Karen cleaned off the breakfast table. Their kitchen was bright and cheery and fresh in the way that new California kitchens should be, Julia decided. The one thing she had hated most about the old house she bought in Pittsley was the dark kitchen. She had been able to tackle, with Adam's help, tearing off the old palm-leaf wallpaper, sanding down the plaster and painting the walls white, taking off the cabinet doors and sanding and repainting all the cabinets a two-tone beige, pulling up the linoleum and replacing it with vinyl tiles that looked like a stone floor, spackling the ceiling, replacing the lighting, and cleaning the old stainless steel sink and faucet until it looked new. But no matter what she did, the kitchen was still too dark and she couldn't fix it herself. She had to have a skylight, even though it wasn't in her budget. Adam had found a local man to do the job at a reasonable price, given that they worked along with him, and thus it was installed. It was her joy now to cook in a kitchen where she could feel the airy daylight. Karen's kitchen was like that.

The sliding door to the porch was open and the morning breeze carried in the salty smell of the Pacific Ocean. Jesse blew bubbles that she wiped away with the corner of his bib. Except for missing Adam, she could not imagine being happier.

"Once upon a time," she said nuzzling the baby, "there was a little rabbit named Fiver who had an older brother named Hazel. And they lived in a warren with miles and miles of underground burrows."

"You used to read that to me when I was little," Karen said affectionately.

"Read what?" asked Paul.

Karen turned to him in surprise. "Don't you know *Watership Down?*"

He shook his head.

"I still have the book. I'll send it to you. Then," Julia added mirthfully, "Karen can read it to both of you."

Paul grinned crookedly as he looked at Karen. "Works for me."

Karen flushed a little and turned to her mother. "I remember all the stories you used to read to me, Mom. That's probably why I became an editor. Actually I was just thinking about writing a children's book." She turned back to Paul. "You could illustrate it, hon. For Jesse. Wouldn't that be fun?"

"Sounds like a great idea. What subject?"

"I'm not sure yet. Maybe about a hummingbird. I've always liked hummingbirds." Karen turned to Julia, the words spilling out in enthusiasm. "We have a species called Rufous hummingbirds, R-u-f-o-u-s—wouldn't that be a good name for our hero, Rufus, R-u-f-u-s? They're only three and a-half inches long," she measured it off with her thumb and index finger, "and their wings beat up to eighty times a second. A second! They like our Canna lilies and we can watch them right off our deck. They migrate through here on their way from Canada to Mexico and back, as much as six-thousand miles each way. Isn't that amazing? They have the most gorgeous red-bronze throats," she put her hand to her own throat, "and their little hearts beat one thousand times a minute. Can you imagine? They're just wonderful little creatures."

Julia and Paul exchanged smiles.

"She gets that way," Paul said, "when she's excited about something."

"I know," Julia replied.

"Well," Karen said apologetically, "I've been reading up on them."

"I love the idea of working on a book with you," Paul said.

Julia tapped her index finger lightly on Jesse's abdomen while making a 'hmmm-m-m-m' hummingbird sound that delighted him.

In the background, the television commercials ended and the news came on. The newscaster began summarizing a virtual tour of the world's events: the unraveling of the war in Iraq; North Korea going nuclear; the Taliban returning to Afghanistan. A volcanic eruption in Indonesia; a hurricane in the Caribbean; a genocide here, a genocide there, everywhere a genocide. Floods, famine, fire, war, disasters of Biblical proportions. Government coups; atrocities; mass graves; bird flu, AIDS, Ebola, and cholera. President Chavez of Venezuela predicting the end of the American Empire. OPEC threatening to turn off the oil spigot. Then the reporter shifted to national news: murders, abductions, rapes, extortion, pollution, and global warming. He gave a litany of the upheavals of the natural order

"I'm so sick of hearing all that," Karen said sharply as she flipped off the sound with the t.v. remote. Then she twisted her long blonde hair into a knot and pinned it up with a plain barrette. "I'd rather think about hummingbirds."

She really was quite pretty, her daughter, Julia observed, even without makeup. Karen got her blonde hair and her height from her father, but she had Julia's own grey eyes and—she flattered herself—her mother's face. She and Paul made an attractive couple. Little Jesse seemed to combine the best of both of them. But of course, she reminded herself, she was besotted with her very first grandchild.

She rocked the baby in her arms, unable to dispel completely the glum effect of the newscaster's report, and she couldn't help wondering what kind of scary world Jesse would inherit. The terrorist attack on the World Trade Center had changed everything. Or perhaps everything had changed long before and this was just the moment they all realized it. The question of the era had become 'Where were you on 9/11?'

She recalled vividly that Tuesday morning. She was alone in the Boston condo where she and Phillip lived, but he had already moved out. She was watching television while having her yogurt before leaving to teach her first class of the day. The program was interrupted (was it The Today Show on NBC? she couldn't remember) to show the smoke coming out of the North Tower. The first speculations were that a private plane had gone off course and slammed into Tower 1. But it was a clear day with perfect visibility and the commentator was wondering how that could have happened. Then just as the smoke and fire seemed too great to be a small plane, she watched a second plane actually come onto the screen from the right, aimed directly at Tower 2. At that instant, there was no doubt that it was deliberate. But even then, no one was saying Al Quaeda.

Her overriding concern had been for her daughter. Karen was working at Harcourt, Inc. on East 26th Street. Although her building wasn't in the Financial District, her apartment was not that far away from the WTC. She frantically dialed her daughter's home number but couldn't get through. All the trunk lines were busy. But somehow, within the next agonizing fifteen minutes, Karen phoned her. "I'm all right, Mom," she said without preamble, "I'm with Paul. We're both okay. I'll talk to you later. Tell Dad I'm okay. I love you." Julia only had time to say, "I love you, too," when the phone cut out. She dialed Phillip's cell number and reached him on the first ring. It was the only time in the past two years she had felt any emotion from him. Despite their estrangement, they cried together in profound relief for their daughter and in abject sorrow for the victims and for the nation.

Shaking off the mood, Julia put her nose to the baby's head and smelled the sweet newborn hair.

"I'm always doing that too," Paul said. "He smells like vanilla pudding. At least *that* end of him."

Julia flashed him a quick grin as she conjured up the memory of her own child as an infant, her only child. Images flooded her mind of weekend mornings when Julia and Phillip would bring their baby to bed with them. They would fall back asleep and doze luxuriously until eventually Karen would stand up holding onto the headboard and rock them awake. Then, more times than Julia could recall, the baby would sit down on her face, or his, with a wet diaper and they would laugh lovingly. It felt like their small bed were a raft in calm waters, cradling their little family together.

But of course that didn't last. She had married Phillip when they were still in graduate school and in time they diverged like two sides of a triangle. They had waited until Karen was through college and on her own before separating. Their stormy divorce was well past now, and they had even managed to be civil at the baptism—probably because he had the good judgment for once not to bring his new Barbie-doll wife to the ceremony.

"I really wish you didn't have to leave today," Karen said.

"Me, too. But, you know," Julia shrugged exaggeratedly, "so many crazies, so little time."

Paul frowned. "Is it really safe, working with mental patients? I know it's a hospital all, but…."

"Don't worry," Julia answered lightly. "They're all medicated into submission." But safe? Nothing really felt safe anymore.

"Would you ever consider moving out here?" Paul asked.

Julia watched his eyes flick over to Karen. Had they colluded over this question and decided he should be the one to ask? They knew she was a pushover for Paul.

After a shaky start, she had come to adore her son-in-law. Karen had met him after she'd moved to New York to become a junior editor at Harcourt. Paul had taken the wedding pictures for Karen's girlfriend, Janet. Karen had been the maid-of-honor. At first, Julia was concerned that he was a man without prospects or ambition. A party photographer. But she decided to trust in Karen's judgment and she was thrilled when Paul turned out to be a highly successful graphic artist. Karen had never doubted it.

"It's been great having you with us," he continued earnestly.

"Oh, sure," she teased, "the mother-in-law jokes will fly after I leave."

"Of course. I got a million of 'em." He pushed a stray lock of brown hair out of his eyes with his wet hand.

"Maybe you could come back for the holidays?" Karen implored.

"I'll try, possum, but I can't promise."

Her finances were stretched pretty thin these days. She had flown out earlier in the year to be with Karen and Paul when Jesse was born and stayed for a week until his baptism. This trip, at least, was combined with her Association meeting. But she wasn't certain she could afford another so soon. She hated the fact that she hadn't been able to help them financially for the down payment on their house last year and begrudgingly thankful that Phillip could.

"It would be nice," her daughter said shyly, "if Adam could come, too. I'd like to meet him."

"I'd like you to meet him. And for him to meet you, and Paul, and Jesse."

"So what is it with you two?" Paul dried his hands on the dishtowel. "Are you going to get married or what?"

"I think it's 'or what,'" Julia answered. "Neither of us are looking for marriage right now."

Paul pretended to put his hands over Jesse's ears. "Not in front of the children," he whispered.

She laughed, but it was faked. She really wasn't sure what her relationship with Adam was. They lived separately but spent most nights together at her house or his. Did she not want to marry him? Or was it the reverse? He had never been married and he seemed the quintessential bachelor. For now they were content, but did they have a future together? And if they didn't, then what?

"All the more reason to meet him," Karen added. "He's got to pass the date-my-mother test." She turned to Julia. "The one you used to use for me, remember?"

"I don't remember any test," Paul said.

"No," Karen replied, "it was too late for you. When I'd have a first date come to the condo to pick me up, she would pretend the garbage disposal was broken just to see how he'd react. If he offered to help, she'd give me a thumbs-up. Otherwise...." She gestured a thumbs-down. "But you'd have passed anyway." She turned back to Julia. "What about Adam?"

"He'd pass," Julia assured her. "But then he'd probably go into the kitchen, disassemble the unit, and replace it with junk parts."

"Just like Dad," Karen said facetiously. Her father was legendary for being absent when anything mechanical needed to be fixed.

Julia laughed again, this time genuinely. She felt the pang of being so far from her family. But this was home for them now. Paul had a studio in Los Angeles and Karen telecommuted as a contract editor for Harcourt in San Diego. As for Julia, she had worked too hard to make the transition from Boston to Pittsley, from teacher to psychologist, and from ex-wife to self-reliant, to build a new life for herself. She had her own home now, but it just happened to be a continent away from theirs.

"You know, you and Phil are the only grandparents that Jesse will ever know," Paul said. His mother had died when he was very young and his father had died of cancer two years before Karen met him.

"Now I feel worse," she said ruefully.

"Good." He made an exaggerated bow. "Then my job here is done."

"And if you don't come back for Christmas," Karen mock-scolded as she refilled their glasses with iced tea, "we just might teach him to call you *Grammie*."

Julia scrunched up her face. "That's lowdown blackmail."

As soon as Karen had announced her pregnancy, Julia emphatically proclaimed she would *not* be called any variation of 'grandma' until she was ninety.

"The means justify the ends," said Paul, his eyes glinting.

All three smiled and looked at each other wistfully.

Three hours later, Julia sat in the LAX departure lounge waiting for her flight to be called. There were two rows of back-to-back orange plastic bucket-chairs on each side of the ticket counter. She automatically scanned the passengers opposite her across the lounge. She did not feel the same comfort in flying that she'd once had. She was mistrustful, but wasn't everybody? She no longer believed she lived in a protected world. But perhaps she never had. Perhaps they all had been blissfully ignorant before that. Now, it constantly felt like they were on the brink of another disaster, pushing ahead with their lives but vulnerable at every turn.

She watched a family of four—a well-dressed young Black couple with two children, a girl around seven and a boy around five, both in Banana Republic khaki shorts and matching yellow tops—waiting in the line at the counter for their seat assignments.

In front of them, a beefy security guard stood next to the counter talking in a low voice on some sort of communication headset. His gaze did not linger on the young family in front of him but instead watched the other waiting passengers as he took in the scope of the airport around him.

The little boy was pulling on his father's hand trying to free himself. The young man grabbed the boy by the belt and hauled him back. The child began to cry.

"Quiet," the father said softly. "Stay still." But the boy would not be quiet and the young man gave his wife a desperate look.

The little girl put her arms around her mother's leg. "I'm tired, Mommy." She kept repeating it until her mother lifted her up and passed her to her father. Meanwhile, the mother took custody of their screaming son, fished in her purse with her free hand and produced a red licorice candy that she held out to the boy. She whispered something to him and he stopped screaming and put out his hand. She gave him the candy, which he promptly popped into his mouth. The man and woman looked at each other in commiseration. Holding his daughter in his arm, the man put his other arm around his wife's waist.

Directly across from Julia sat an elderly Mexican woman. She wore a long multicolored flared skirt, laced black shoes with thick stacked heels, a cherry-colored sweater over a white blouse, and a multicolored kerchief with the same colors as in the skirt but in a different pattern. She sat turned away with her head down and her arms folded over her black handbag.

Julia couldn't help staring at her. At first, it was simply the stare of not knowing where else to look. Then, it was out of curiosity. Something didn't fit. Was it that the woman didn't move? Didn't look up? What was it about her that seemed odd? Maybe it was the way she sat with her knees apart, feet squarely on the tiled floor. Or that her hands, what Julia could see of them, seemed larger than they should be. Something was off, that much she knew. Should she say anything to the guard? He would probably think she was paranoid. Was she?

Still undecided, she got up from her seat and began walking toward the guard. But as she neared him, she saw two men in grey sanitation jumpsuits flank the seated woman. One of them spoke to her in a soft voice. The other man held his hand in his pocket. The woman looked around furtively. At that moment, Julia was certain it was not a woman and she was quite certain the two men were not sanitation workers. The men elevated the imposter out of his seat and escorted him from the lounge without incident.

"What was that all about?" Julia asked the guard in as innocuous a tone as she could muster.

"All what about?"

"Removing that person."

"I have no idea." He answered in a monotone but his eyes betrayed him.

It took forever to board the plane. Security was tighter than ever but nothing was mentioned about apprehending anyone.

Finally airborne, Julia tried to evoke the fragrance of Jesse's baby hair to calm herself down but it was soon replaced by the turgid smell of the airplane mixed with the odors of food from the galley. She ordered a gin and tonic to help her sleep during the flight. It didn't work.

It was noisy in coach. Somewhere in back, a young child was fretting. Behind her was a soccer team of young men who kept up a steady stream of boisterous banter. Across the aisle to her left was a young Latino couple. She noticed that they had both crossed themselves upon take-off.

The seats next to her were occupied by two young women who were deep in conversation about their upcoming plans in Boston. Apparently one was starting a job at the Museum of Fine Arts in the collections department. She was a seascape artist, she said, and was looking forward to going to Gloucester and Rockport to paint the fishing boats. She'd had a gallery exhibit in San Francisco and was hoping for the same in Boston. The darker-haired woman was returning home from visiting her boyfriend, a film editor at MGM. She was a filmmaker too, making a small independent movie about a coastal village in Maine. They seemed oblivious to Julia.

They're so eager and capable, Julia thought. So young and innocent of mortality. And, thinking that, she couldn't help being reminded of her best friend, Tessa Jensen. Tessa the musician, Tessa wife and mother, Tessa full of life and laughter. They had become as close as sisters ever since Julia had moved to Pittsley. When Tessa had a lumpectomy for breast cancer two years ago, it had seemed as though nothing could have been more unfair. This was a woman younger than herself, who had never owned a party dress or a new stove or even a frivolous lipstick. She was a woman who went to bed tired and got up tired every day. She worked full-time teaching music to high school students, managed the household chores and all the finances, took care of a blind husband and a teenage son, and never even complained about her migraines. But it wasn't the cancer that killed her eight months ago. It was a massive stroke and heart attack. It had shocked Julia to the core. What is the point of optimism, Julia thought, if someone so deserving could die so abruptly?

But that was at least a comprehensible death. Tessa was ill and her heart failed. Whereas Julia's grandparents' deaths had not been comprehensible. She had spent summers with them on their farm in Quebec Province every year until the sixth grade when her parents told her that they had died but didn't tell her how until she was in high school. They'd been senselessly murdered by a serial killer. She didn't learn her grandmother had been raped until years later. She'd admitted to herself that their murder was probably the reason she became a psychologist. And that led her to teaching psychology, something she'd never truly enjoyed. If it hadn't been for Dr. Sam, she might still be teaching some tedious introductory Psych course. She'd met him three years ago when she began visiting Tully's son at the mental hospital. They'd finally diagnosed Tommy as a high-functioning autistic.

Her mind then drifted back again to her grandparents and she began to feel that old sorrow that sometimes came over her. She forced herself instead to visualize her grandpère's twinkling brown eyes when he smiled at her, and her grandmère's long blonde hair which had skipped two generations—her mother and her—only to show up in Karen. Of course Phillip contributed that gene as well. And from there, she thought of her parents. How they would have loved to see their great-grandchild. How sad that they were gone too.

Enough of that, she rebuked herself. I'm getting morbid. I've got other things to think about right now. Practical things. The most pressing of which was: Should she leave her position at Bridgewater State Psychiatric Hospital and go into private practice with Dr. Raymond Alonzo? He was expecting her answer when she got back.

Alonzo, as he preferred to be called, told her he was going to leave McLean Hospital in Belmont to go into community psychiatry in New Bedford. Julia had met him through the transfer of her patient, Cheryl Fayette, from Bridgewater to a research project in the upscale Harvard-affiliated McLean Hospital. That he asked her to join him—her, a mere psychologist at a second-string psychiatric institution—was an offer she hadn't expected.

His practice would focus on adolescents. She would be dealing with kids from abusive homes, with drug addiction, violence, depression and suicidal tendencies, as well as with children from some fairly intractable economic disadvantages. It would be remedial psychology but without the hospital structure. There didn't seem to be any overwhelming incentive to make the change except that she respected Alonzo and knew she could learn a lot from him. Plus she would be more autonomous. But was this the direction she wanted to go in? By the time she arrived in Boston, she had still hadn't made up her mind.

* * *

By speeding up Route 24 and onto the Southeast Expressway, Adam arrived at Logan just in time for Julia to disembark the plane. He had spent the previous hour, along with the police, bog workers, and volunteers, combing the woods for B.J.'s friend Ponlok. At the time he left for the airport, they still hadn't found the lost boy and were still searching. Maybe they had located him by now. He'd find out as soon as they got home.

Adam caught sight of Julia amidst the crowd of people bulging out of the arrival gate. She stood out in a lime-green silk blouse and cream-colored skirt with her shoulder-length chestnut hair bouncing as she walked briskly in high-heels towards him. She was tanned and her hair glinted with steaks of California sunshine. As soon as he caught her eye, she smiled broadly. For a woman nearing fifty, she was decidedly stunning.

"He's absolutely beautiful," Julia was enthusiastically telling him as they inched their way out of the airport in Adam's truck and back onto the Expressway. He listened dutifully to her ardent description of her grandson and her visit with Karen and Paul.

"You just have to see him," Julia continued. "I'd like to go back around Christmas. Do you think you could come with me? We'd have a wonderful time. Go to San Francisco. Drive up the coast. It's spectacular. What do you think?"

"Sure," Adam said. No point in arguing when she's just come home. After all, that was nearly three months away.

"Really?"

"Sure."

"Wonderful!" She rested her hand lightly on his thigh. "You'll love it there."

But privately he was wondering if perhaps Julia had come to love it there a little too much. Was she considering moving there to be with her daughter? Did she want to convince him to move there too?

As they traveled south towards Pittsley, Adam felt a wave of relief to be out of Boston. The traffic was monstrous. The corrupt Big Dig (Big Hole, Mole Hole, Damn Scam—the nicknames were endless and all disparaging) that was supposed to have streamlined the commute only worsened it with dark, leaky tunnels, cryptic signage, and a Kafkaesque journey under the city. Could anyone drive through the tunnel anymore, he wondered, without being reminded that a woman had been crushed to death when a three-ton concrete ceiling panel fell on her without warning?

There was a time he had liked coming into the city, but lately it seemed like too much effort. There was no civility there now. He appreciated the small amenities of country living where he could find a parking space wherever he needed to go, people tended to be courteous because it wasn't overcrowded, and the pace of life didn't require a wristwatch. It was the way he preferred it, even though it wasn't idyllic. Nothing was ever completely idyllic. Like today.

And so, after Julia had exhausted the topic of her fabulous grandson, he began telling her about the disappearance of the Cambodian boy from the cranberry bog.

Julia shook her head thoughtfully as he finished. "I have a weird feeling about this, Adam. It reminds me of the little Bradburn girl. And we never did find out who all the other men were in that cult."

Three years ago, Julia had found Jeannine Bradburn's butchered body in Pittsley Woods. And from that, she and Adam had discovered the cult killings of other little girls in the area. But while Jeannine's killers—Floyd Mather and Babe Hampley—were both dead, there were other members of the cult who had never been identified.

"They only abducted young girls," Adam reminded her.

"I know. But it troubles me. I mean, how is it that we have another disappearance of a child in Pittsley? It's too small a country town for that."

He had to agree. But it didn't have the same characteristics of the other disappearances. If the cult wanted girls, why would they take a boy?

"He just got lost in the woods," Adam said. "They've probably found him by now."

Traffic was thinning out as they passed Brockton. Slowly the landscape altered into fewer commercial buildings and shopping malls into intermittent high-banked wooded areas. He began to feel calmer.

By the time they reached the outskirts of town, the road was reduced to two lanes, lined with overarching trees like the entrance to a plantation. The sun had set and the clear night sky was riddled with stars. Turning onto the dirt road where Adam lived, the houses increasingly spread out like the ribs of an unfolding fan.

Adam's house appeared rather ordinary with grey cedar shakes and olive green window trim. It was a small structure, the upstairs with only a large bedroom and bathroom and the downstairs with just a livingroom, half-bath, and kitchen. There was no sign in front to announce a veterinary clinic, not even an arrow to direct people to the back of the house where they would enter through the basement door into a fully equipped modern facility. No sign was necessary; people in Pittsley already knew where to bring their animals.

There were no streetlights to dim the brilliant stars. Getting out of the pick-up, they both paused for a moment, leaning up against the truck bed to look at the constellations and the waxing moon as the crickets and cicadas chirped a loud continuous chorus. The night air had turned crisp, too cold for Julia's summery blouse. Adam put his arm around her shoulder and pulled her next to him. He felt her chilly arm and rubbed it gently to warm her. Then he took off his camouflage Army jacket and put it around her shoulders.

"I guess I don't have any imagination," Julia remarked looking upward. "All I can ever find is the Big Dipper."

"I bet most people can't identify the constellations. I think we should just make up our own. That one, for instance," Adam pointed to the west, "that's Goody sitting in his rocker. Those are his knobby knees and he's holding his shotgun."

"I see that," she said wryly.

"You don't find a constellation like that in California." After he said it, he wondered where that had come from. Was he jealous of a place?

"It's hard to see anything with the smog sometimes," Julia answered. "But it's lovely out over the ocean."

"*We* have an ocean."

"Yes."

"Not that far from here."

"No, not far," she agreed looking up at him with one corner of her mouth upturned just a little, not quite a smile. Then she turned her head slightly and he could just imagine her arching her right eyebrow.

Pittsley, in fact, was miles inward from the Atlantic but less than a fifteen-minute drive to New Bedford Harbor, the commercial fishing capital of New England. Twenty minutes to Plymouth Harbor and the *Mayflower* and *Plimouth Plantation* replicas. Forty minutes to Cape Cod. Much of the history of the Massachusetts colonial settlement was right here. Adam decided he could never relate to the Pacific in the same way. Could she?

Entering the house, Catastrophe's tail wagged boundlessly and she jumped up like a puppy at seeing her mistress. Julia hugged her tightly while Adam made a phone call to the police chief. The news was not good.

"Burke says they haven't found him yet," he told Julia after he hung up. "They'll start searching again in the morning."

The alarm on her face matched the feeling in his stomach. "Does he still think the boy is just lost?"

"It's what he wants to think," Adam answered.

After dropping off Cat and her luggage at Julia's house, and waiting for Julia to grab a jacket, Adam headed for Dottie's Restaurant. It was the only actual restaurant in town, Dud's Suds being primarily a tavern although the pub grub was quite good there.

The one-room eatery was nearly full, with a twelve-stool counter space, square tables in the center, and booths along the sides. Adam and Julia got the last booth. Dottie had recently redecorated the restaurant with mirrors and a pink-and-black motif. The cook, Chester, her husband and partner for over twenty years, took the opportunity to add a new dish to his repertoire of broiled fish, pot roast, salmon loaf, liver and onions, turkey platter, roasted chicken, pizza, and pork chops Italiano. He'd recently become enamored of cacoila, a spiced pork butt, and had added the Portuguese sandwich to the menu. It was a major event in his culinary life. The fragrance of garlic, onion, and paprika floated out from the kitchen.

Amidst the background buzz of a dozen conversations, Dottie wedged her amble bulk between them and the adjacent table and said loudly, "Hi, you two, do you want a menu, or the usual?"

They ordered a large pizza, half anchovy for Julia. A beer for Adam, diet soda for her. The usual.

"Haven't seen you in a couple of weeks, Julia," Dottie said as she wrote down their order on her pad.

"I was visiting my grandchild. In California."

"Oh yeah? I hope you're not going to pull out photos because then I'd have to pull out mine and you guys would never get your food," she cackled.

"No photos," Julia chuckled, "only for myself. I know how it is with baby pictures. You get demerits if you don't say they're gorgeous."

"I tried to pass off my granddaughter as my own kid but nobody believed it." Dottie winked. "So, if I'll tell you you're not old enough to be a grandmother will you do the same for me?"

"Done," said Julia.

"Me, too, if it will get us our dinner quicker," Adam joked.

Dottie shook a finger at him. "Be nice to your waitress or she'll spit in your food." Then she inclined her bleached-blonde head towards a table in the corner. "By the way, I hear the Juckets talking about losing their land. What's that all about, Adam?"

Jucket was the term everyone used, even Juckets themselves, for the diminishing backwoods community on the edge of town. They were still, by tradition, a little lawless and rowdy. They lived in a rabbit-warren of small houses insulated from the rest of the town and even when they went out for entertainment, they kept mostly to themselves.

"I don't know, Dottie," he answered truthfully, "but I'll nose around."

"Good," she said. "Your folks need some help."

The 'your folks' was a circumstance Adam had grown up with.

Although his father was Polish, his mother was a Wombart so he was always considered at least half-Jucket. (Tully was full-blown, but even the Juckets considered him a bubble-off-plumb.)

"What's going on?" Julia asked him after Dottie left.

"I'm not sure. But I wonder if it's the same thing that's happening to Tully."

Adam proceeded to fill her in on Tully's plight. Julia expressed the same doubt about the use of eminent domain that Billy had, and was equally shocked to learn that Tully really *could* lose his house and all of his land.

"In New London," Adam explained, "most of the people caved in and agreed to some compensation for their homes. The hold-outs got nothing. You know what Tully's house is like, if he doesn't agree to sell, they'll probably condemn it."

Constructed of plywood and beaverboard, Tully's house hadn't been painted in decades, the roof was in disrepair, and the cedar shakes had dried out and turned mud brown. Inside was no better. Doris, sweet and simple, had never been able to grasp the utility of soap and water on either the kitchen or the kids (all of whom had been removed by the State for neglect years ago). It wasn't much, but it was all they had. Even if Tully got compensation for it, he couldn't afford to buy another home, not in Massachusetts.

"What's he going to do, Adam?"

"He can't handle anything like that. He doesn't know how serious it is. Maybe I should contact Kip."

Max Kipper had defended Tully in the arraignment when the police erroneously thought Tully had murdered Jeannine Bradburn. Not only was Kip a lawyer and a friend, he grew up in Pittsley. If anyone could help he could—even if Adam had to remind Kip occasionally that he started out as a Jucket too.

Later that evening in Julia's king-size bed, fresh from her shower washing off residue of the West Coast, they made love with the passion of absence. She moaned with a catch in her breath as Adam stroked her breasts and slid his hand over her stomach down between her legs.

Instantly they were moving together in a familiar way, both ardent and urgent. Afterwards as they lay naked on the bed wrapped in each other's arms, they both giggled at the sheer joy of being together again.

"But look at my pizza belly," Julia said, rolling over and pointing to the slight bulge in her stomach.

"I think it's sexy." Adam traced sensuous circles around her navel.

"Where were you when I was pregnant?"

Idly, he wondered what kind of father he would have made. Did he regret not having a child? Maybe. Too late now. Adam stared at the ceiling.

"I'm going to go back to the bog tomorrow morning to help them look for Ponlok. Do you want to come?" he said. He knew she hadn't scheduled any appointments with patients until the afternoon.

"I can't. I have a meeting with Raymond Alonzo."

"Oh. Have you made up your mind yet?"

"Not yet."

She got up to use the bathroom first and he watched her walk her jaunty walk knowing full well he was staring at her ass. And a very nice one it was, too, he deemed.

As he looked out of the bedroom window, he could see the half-moon brightly shining. At least the woods wouldn't be completely dark tonight. If the boy were in there, perhaps he wouldn't be so frightened in the moonlight.

* * *

He awoke in a darkened room. Where? He remembered being in the cranberry bog. Remembered going into the woods to pee. Then someone was behind him, holding a cloth over his nose and mouth. He struggled helplessly as he breathed something strong. It all went blank. He'd been kidnapped. Why? And what would his mother think?

He imagined her standing now in front of the small wooden cabinet she'd placed on the table beside her bed, the other occupants of the room politely turned away so that she might have privacy. She would slowly unfold a red cotton cloth revealing a polished sandalwood statue. The caramel-colored Buddha sat in the cross-legged position with his right hand elevated, palm outward in a gesture of peace and protection. Aside from their few clothes, this was the only thing they'd brought with them from Cambodia.

His father, Nisay, had left them behind ten years ago after he lost his job in a small textile factory to the boss's son. He went to Phnom Penh to look for work in a larger garment factory that made jeans for The Gap in America. Ponlok and his mother went to live with her sister and brother-in-law to wait for him. When they heard from her cousin that his father was gambling and going to sex workers, they knew he wouldn't come back. Then they heard that he was sick from AIDS, and then they heard no more. Her sister and brother-in-law had three children and couldn't afford to keep them any longer. So when the uncle told his mother about coming to America, she said 'yes.' She gave the uncle what little money she had from selling her sewing and embroidery. Their family contributed the rest to make up his fee.

At least here there was work, she told him. During the week—while he was in summer school and now in regular school—his mother laid interlocking pine boards at her uncle's hardwood flooring company. Of course, he wasn't actually her uncle, but rather the expediter who brought them into the U.S. six months ago. He put them in a small third-story apartment with twenty other Cambodians—most of them right there in that bog.

Didn't they see him? Didn't they look for him?

He heard men's voices nearby, he couldn't tell how many. Coming from outside the door.

"What the hell were you thinking? It's a boy, not a girl. Why in hell did you snatch a **boy**?"

"I didn't know it was a boy. It looked like a girl."

"What the hell are we going to do with him? And what are we going to tell Usha?"

Monday, October 2nd

At dawn, police car after police car drove up the dirt road to the cranberry bog, spraying plumes of dust into the air behind them. Adam followed them, with B.J., who was excused from school for the day, in the passenger side of his truck. Behind him came five other pick-up trucks and ten SUVs filled with Pittsley volunteers.

How many of the same people, Adam wondered, had turned out to search for Jeannine Bradburn three years ago in that cold January? They hadn't found her, not until Julia and Cat stumbled across the half-buried body in the woods four months later. Jeannine's body hadn't been there when they originally scoured Pittsley Woods. Day after day they'd searched, then convinced themselves that she was a runaway, all of them laden with guilt when she turned up dead. No one could bear to think it might happen again. The faces of these volunteers were grim with that memory. There were no rallying cries of "Let's find him, folks!" or "Look sharp! He's out there waiting for us!"

The temperature had dropped into the low fifties overnight but the erratic Indian Summer was expected to revert to a normal autumn day in the low seventies. The morning sun had just risen and was beginning to burn off the dew on the bog. To Adam, it was a parfait of sun, sky, trees, and low-lying mist.

Then he saw Chaya Nim standing on the edge of the bog as though she were alone on a distant planet. She must have been dropped off there by someone, perhaps the man who organized the workers. She was holding a photograph and what looked like a white shirt.

Police Chief Burke approached her first, towering over the small woman. Adam was glad that Carson Burke had decided to make Pittsley home. He'd gotten off to a hard start with most of the Force thinking he was just another yuppie transplant. "Chief Jerk" people had called him behind his back. But now, three years later, he was every bit as comfortable in his role as if he'd been a country cop all his life. He even looked the part after giving up his tailored suits and expensive shoes.

Burke said something to the distraught woman that she obviously didn't understand, but it was nevertheless clear that they were all here to help her look for her son. She offered him the photo and the shirt, then put her palms together in front of her chest and bowed to all of them. Tears of gratitude poured over the banks of her eyes like the rising Mekong.

The Chief passed the photo around to everyone with a description of what the boy was wearing. The tracking dogs came out of the van, five of them, a mixed group of German Shepherds and mongrels, all wagging their tails in eager anticipation of a job to do. Adam heard Burke tell the handlers that the mother had brought Ponlok's shirt for the dogs to sniff. She had gestured that she had washed it good. She was proud to present him with such a clean shirt.

The K-9 handler in charge shook his head. "We're not going to get very good smells from that. Is that all she has?"

Three hours later, they still had not found any trace of Ponlok and Adam had to leave to check in at his clinic.

Only one patient was waiting for him today. Charlie Boyd brought in his nine-year-old boxer-cross, who lay on his side in the waiting room, his brown body stretched out the length of two chairs. Boyd never brought in Fred except for his annual rabies shots. Fred's job was to bark when anyone came into the yard and he was kept chained to his doghouse except for the coldest days when Charlie would take him into the basement. There wasn't anything illegal about chaining a dog and Charlie always made sure Fred had food, water, and adequate shelter. And in his own way, he quite cared for the dog.

"He won't get up," Charlie said, taking off his cap and running his hand over his bulbous forehead and through his pale hair which, in his mid-thirties, was already thinning out.

"How did you get him here?" Adam asked.

"Lifted him up, put him in the truck, and carried him in."

Fred had to weigh a good hundred pounds and Charlie couldn't go much more than one-fifty himself, Adam thought as he bent down and examined the dog in place.

"You been giving him the heartworm pills?" Fred was wearing a flea and tick collar and didn't have any noticeable ticks on him.

"Every month," Charlie said.

Fred looked up at him with clear soulful eyes and licked Adam's hand. In palpating the dog, Adam couldn't find any tender areas that the dog reacted to until he moved Fred's hind legs. At that, the dog whimpered.

"Anything unusual happen to Fred lately?" he asked.

Charlie thought a moment. "Well, he got off his chain yesterday. Might have gotten into something he shouldn't. You think he got poisoned?"

"Where'd he go?"

"Just in and out of the woods across the street. He ran around like a hound for about two hours before he came back."

Adam stood up.

"Is he going to die, doc?"

"No, Charlie, he isn't going to die. Fred is just exhausted. He's nine and his muscles and joints hurt because he never gets any exercise and he ran around for two hours. He overdid it, that's all. He was glad to be loose. Wouldn't you be?"

The small man dropped his eyes guiltily down to his dog. "I guess."

"I'm going to give him a shot that will give him some relief right away. It'll ease the inflammation and help with the pain. And I'll give you some pills to give him twice a day, morning and night. When he's feeling better, you're going to have to walk him for a half-hour every day. Then you're going to increase it. You'll rig up a line across the yard that you can put him on so he can exercise all day."

Charlie nodded, chastened.

After treating the dog, and lecturing Charlie some more about exercise, Adam helped him get Fred back into the truck.

"Thanks, doc. I'm partial to him, you know. But he ain't no hunter, that's for sure."

"Boxers aren't."

"Yeah, instead of a coon or something, all he brings back yesterday is a shower shoe." He patted the dog in the bed of the truck. "At least you tried, fella."

"A shower shoe?"

"Yeah, see?" He pointed in the bed of the truck where a green flip-flop lay amongst a pile of rakes, shovels, and two trash bags. "I just threw it in there 'til I get to the dump."

Charlie's house was on the other side of the road from Amos Hall's bog. Adam instantly thought of Ponlok Nim. "Mind if I take this?"

Charlie looked at him askance. "Help yourself."

As Adam retrieved the flip-flop from the truck, he saw Charlie glance down at his feet. The man was probably wondering, Adam decided, if the vet was going to wear it.

When Adam went back inside his office, he found a message on his answering machine.

"Amos Hall. Call back."

Adam had known Amos since they were classmates together in grammar school. Amos was always in the top of the class, but even as a boy, he'd measured his words and seldom were any extra spoken over a telephone. And since Amos didn't keep animals, Adam assumed it had to do with the disappearance of the Cambodian boy. Maybe there was some good news.

"Did they find the boy?" Adam asked when he returned the call.

"No," replied Amos.

"What's up then?"

"You should come over."

Amos' house was on the other side of Pittsley Center, about four miles west. It was originally a farmhouse built in the 1800s and Amos was fastidious about maintaining it. The front door was solid oak with iron hinges and a well-turned doorknocker with the initial "H."

"Come in, I have something to ask you." Amos greeted Adam at the door with his reading glasses still perched at the end of his nose, his hands gripping a certified letter. He was almost as tall as Adam and just as lithe, but he looked older than his years. His once-brown hair was fully streaked with white and his thin face showed the ravaging effects of sun and wind. "They want to take my land away. On a pretext of eminent domain. Not my birthright, they won't, no sir."

The man standing in front of Adam was the tenth generation of Halls on that bog and in that house. The Hall property once covered several hundred acres but in his grandparents' time, some of the land was sold off. Amos' father had kept five bogs, including the one next to Lake Tispisquin. The family had been well-to-do, philanthropic to the town over the years, and upstanding citizens, all of them. Amos was the last of the line, never married and no siblings.

With all his money, Adam reckoned that until today Amos' main worry was focused on insects. Between the cold spring, dry summer, and wet autumn, the dreaded fireworm had resurfaced in some unpredictable cycle and had aborted a portion of the buds that became cranberries. The bogs would only harvest half the usual crop. And even if were a full harvest, the market for cranberries was becoming saturated.

Although Massachusetts produced nearly two million barrels per year (second only to Wisconsin, which produced three and a-half), demand was not significantly increasing in the U.S. The industry had turned its face to international expansion. Just about everything that could be done with cranberries had been done. Sauce, juice, jam, baking products, dried berries, cranberry oil, cranberry candles, cranberry ice cream, white cranberry juice (using the unripe berry)—there wasn't much left to invent. Had they exhausted the cranberry? And how did such a bitter fruit become the Commonwealth's most lucrative agricultural product anyway? They all knew it was just a serendipitous combination of marketing and history.

Cranberry bogs in Massachusetts had been formed in peatlands and outwash of kettleholes eons after the Laurentine ice sheet melted. Along with the glacial retreat came the detritus of everything from boulders to sand and gravel. Stones pushed up sharply through the ground like perennial bulbs, and proliferated like crocuses, daffodils, or tulips, or they lay just under the surface waiting to be plowed up like turnips or potatoes. No wonder that the settlers of Plymouth Bay Colony had called it rock farming. And although wild cranberries were well known to the Indians and introduced to the colonists, they did not cultivate them. That didn't happen until the mid-1800s. The names Hall and Howes, Hathaway, and Lovell were among the first cranberry growers in this region.

Now, some of the newer bog owners were allowing the bogs to go fallow while the owners waited until the vines died and the land became usable again to harvest 'gravel berries' rather than Howes, Early Blacks, and Centennials—gravel having become more profitable than *Viccinium macrocarpon* in this age of construction and development. Not so, however, Amos Hall. He would never give in to squandering his heritage, Adam knew, even if he had to take a loss again this year.

Inside his colonial-style livingroom, Amos faced Adam with a determined look. "I need you to call your lawyer friend, Max Kipper. Phone's over there. I already spoke to the Association. This will not stand."

Within the hour, six other men and one woman sat in Amos' modest livingroom on straight-back chairs with woven-rush seats while Adam read them the letter from the town attorney.

"And," added Amos when Adam had finished, "if they take my bog now, they can take yours later. They can take anything, anytime they want. Possession, deeds, history, all usurped." He stared at them over his glasses, each of his bushy white eyebrows standing up over his eyes like snow on a mountaintop, uttering more words together than anyone remembered.

What the other bog men were thinking privately did not show on their faces. But Adam knew them to be a stoic lot.

"They're wetlands," Fiona Hathaway finally said, invoking the sacred conservation word. Her people on her mother's side were bog men of a different sort. Bog-trotters was actually what they'd been called in Ireland—after the bog ponies that carted out the peat—before modern 'bog trotting' became a nature-pastime for the British leisure class. Like their New England counterparts, the raised bogs of Shannon were formed in the hollows of glacial moraines, but acid vegetation was the crop rather than cranberries. And rather than fruit, they harvested fuel. Even though her cranberry bogs were inherited from her now-deceased husband, Fiona did not appear daunted by being the only woman in the room; she came from a tradition surpassing theirs.

"The bogs are protected," added Isaac Lovell, as though Amos were overreacting to a nonexistent problem.

"We called the Attorney General's Office." Adam spoke slowly for emphasis, for what he was about to say would change everything. "Wetlands are not exempt from eminent domain."

One by one, their faces slackened.

"Are you sure?" Fionna passed her hand over the brick-red hair that was showing observable strands of grey.

"Positive."

"But why *your* bog?" Isaac asked turning to Amos.

"I don't know."

Neither did Adam. Although he was gradually beginning to piece it together, he wasn't ready to voice his suspicions yet, not until he knew more.

"What can we can possibly do about it?" Enoch Marshall was asking. "You need a lawyer."

"I have one." Amos glanced in acknowledgment towards Adam. "But what I want is the Cranberry Association to stand behind me."

They were, in the way of business, fierce competitors even though they were part of the Association that sold their berries to a single processor, SeaSpray. But they had known each other and their families since childhood. To these particular individuals, bogging was more than just a living. It was living history. With the exception of Fiona, the men in this room were direct descendants of those original bog men.

"Are you with me?"

"Whatever we can do, Amos," said Fiona, and the others nodded assent.

* * *

Thankfully, Julia thought, even though Adam had gotten up and left before dawn he had let her sleep. She'd been barely aware of him moving around the bedroom, hearing the shower. She recalled the sound of the refrigerator door opening and closing as Cat jumped off the bed and padded her way downstairs to freeload a snack before breakfast. Adam must have turned the heat on for her; she could hear the sound of the furnace. It had gotten unexpectedly cold during the night. She was glad she didn't have to be in her office until mid-afternoon and didn't have to be in Belmont until later in the morning. Rolling over and spreading out in her own bed felt like a luxury this morning.

She slept until eight o'clock, abruptly awakened by a jerk of her leg muscles and a fleeting sense of panic. She had been dreaming about walking on a swaying bridge in some remote place, not a jungle, but some place she couldn't recognize. She had begun falling.

She resisted the impulse to attach the dream to anything in particular and went about showering and dressing. After checking the indoor-outdoor thermometer in the window—it read fifty-nine degrees outside—she chose a chocolate-brown slacks' suit and white silk long-sleeved blouse. She re-set the thermostat from sixty-five back down to fifty so the heat would stay off during the day. She would have to economize on her heating bill this winter. It was too high last year and with everything happening in the Middle East now, who knew what this season's prices would be? All summer, gas prices had been up and down, but up higher than ever before and never down to where they had been only a year ago. She was seriously thinking about putting a woodstove into the fireplace for additional heat. But that would be another expense she couldn't really afford.

Adam had left the coffeepot on for her, so she poured herself a cup and grabbed a yogurt while making breakfast for Cat. Then she let out the dog, kissed her on the nose when she came in, and set off for Belmont to meet with Dr. Raymond Alonzo. Backing out of the driveway, she swerved just in time to miss a small chipmunk scurrying across the lawn with a hickory nut in his mouth.

"Watch out, little guy," she said as he scampered up the stone wall in the front of her house and disappeared into a crevice.

As Chief of Staff at McLean, Dr. Alonzo had achieved everything he wanted to do in a psychiatric institution. But that institution served a particular clientele and he wanted, at this stage of his life, to help the disadvantaged. He was ready, he'd told her, for private practice. In other words, he was prepared for a pay-cut.

His proposal to Julia, however, would actually entail an increase in her salary. He said he liked her work, liked the way she had treated Cheryl Fayette (Julia's transfer patient from Bridgewater) and he liked that her supervisor, his friend Dr. Shing Wu, Sam, thought well of her. And he wanted a competent female associate. It didn't matter that she was Caucasian and many of his new clients, like himself, would be Azorean. She would be working with kids of all stripes in New Bedford because the city was multiracial.

The autonomy was both attractive and frightening. Right now, the hospital she worked in provided a safety net. Sam was always there to help her. He was the only person who had seen the clinical psychologist lurking within the psychology professor she had once been. If it hadn't been for Sam, she wouldn't have changed careers. Then, she admonished herself, shouldn't she be more loyal?

"Have you made a decision yet, Julia?"

Alonzo, as he preferred to be called, sat behind the large mahogany desk in his sumptuous McLean office. Framed diplomas, certifications, and awards filled the wall over his head, but the pictures in front of him were all of family. His wife, three sons and two daughters were photographed skiing, ice skating, playing hoop and soccer across his desk. In the only picture that included him, a young Dr. Alonzo and his wife were being pelted with snowballs by all five children and everyone was laughing. Who, Julia wondered, took the picture?

"Honestly, no," Julia replied. "I've given it a lot of thought, but I need a little more time to sort things out."

He rested his elbow on the desk and his chin on his hand. "Would you like to see the new offices? You can pick whatever one you like for your own."

"Is this a bribe?" she said skeptically with a smile.

Alonzo chuckled. "I'm not above bribery. Do it with my patients all the time. Let's take a ride."

They drove separately down to Bridgewater where she left her car in the hospital parking lot, so he could drop her back off there on his return trip. His car was a new red Mercedes-Benz S-class. She raised an inquisitive eyebrow at it as she got in.

"Don't worry, I won't be driving this to work. Marilyn and I are trading cars. She gets this one and I get her PT-Cruiser to take into the city. She's very pleased with the deal."

"Another bribe?"

Alonzo broke out into a baritone guffaw as they turned onto the highway. "Am I that transparent?"

"You gave yourself away."

"So I did," he said appreciatively, "and you nailed me."

He turned onto Route 140 past the Silver City Galleria and through Lakeville, cruising at the speed limit.

"Is that a seat warmer?" Julia asked as she examined at the dashboard.

"Left and right." He pointed at the two buttons. "Try it."

In seconds, she felt the heat penetrating her back. The morning was still chilly even though it would warm up later in the day. She leaned her head back against the leather headrest, the warmth relaxing her muscles, curling into her back, stoking her spine. She let out a deep sigh.

Alonzo turned on his seat warmer. "There's something that happens when you're over fifty. The heat starts feeling really good, doesn't it?"

Julia stuck out her chin. "I'm not over fifty." She pulled away from the seat and turned off the button.

"Did I hit a nerve?" he asked.

She smiled self-deprecatingly. "I became a grandmother a few months ago."

"I know that feeling," he commiserated.

"But in the photos on your desk, your children are all young."

"Ancient history," he conceded. "Caroline, our oldest, is married with two children. I remember the first time my daughter referred to me as

'Grandpa,' I went home and drank four fingers of my best Scotch. Marilyn went out and bought a new wardrobe."

"I like Marilyn's solution."

"You'd like my wife, and she'd like you. You'll have to come to dinner."

As they drove up Johnny Cake Hill, they passed vacant storefronts and very few people shopping. The city looked like it was struggling—parts of it still vibrant and beating, keeping the moribund parts barely alive.

New Bedford was an old city, founded in the 1600s, but the moving religious body wasn't the Puritans but rather the Society of Friends, and the Quakers remained an active force throughout the whaling years. Even today, one could see the liveliness of the meetinghouse on Spring Street. New Bedford still considered itself a maritime city but over the centuries, the face of the city had changed. Many of the houses that had once belonged to affluent whaling captains now belonged either to private organizations, museums, social service agencies, or funeral parlors. The economy, once dependent on industry—which had left for southern climes—and the fishing fleet—now regulated to protect the fish stocks—had taken a downturn in the fifties and continued to slide. What the city hadn't lost, however, was its population. There were still over 90,000 inhabitants with new waves of immigrants following one upon another. The Portuguese had been the strongest contingent for many decades, but recently their primacy was being challenged by Latinos and the influx of Guatemalans, many of whom went to work in the fish plants.

"What New Bedford needs is a vision," Alonzo said as he pulled to the curb in front of one of the empty buildings. "There's potential here with the Harbor and the docks, and so much history. It could be revitalized if only—," he stopped himself. "Don't mind me, I grew up here."

"I thought you came from Mattapoisett," Julia said with surprise. She knew from Sam that Alonzo's home was in that upscale shore community.

"We live there, but Marilyn and I both come from 'New Beffod.'" He deliberately pronounced the name like a local.

As they walked into the building, Julia felt she knew now what was behind his determination to come back. Good for him, she thought. It made her like him all the more.

They spent the next half-hour walking through what he envisioned to be their offices. 'Alonzo and Associates,' he acknowledged, would take a fair amount of remodeling.

"Why don't you ever use your first name?" Julia now felt comfortable enough to ask him a personal question.

He chuckled more to himself than to her. "That *is* my first name. Alonzo Raymond Alonzo. You can imagine what it was like growing up in a tough neighborhood around here with the moniker Alonzo Alonzo."

On the ride back, he eyed her. "You're not an easy sell, are you?"

"It's not that," she replied quickly. "It's a big commitment for me."

They rode on in silence for several miles. Finally, he said, "You're very quiet. Is there something wrong?"

She looked out the window at the passing landscape of highway stores. "I was thinking about the young boy who disappeared from a cranberry bog in Pittsley yesterday."

"Disappeared?"

She relayed as much as she knew Ponlok's vanishing and her concern that there had been a number of other children who'd disappeared in the area in past and were later found dead.

"Wasn't Sherry Fayette's mother from a town near here?" he asked. After Cheryl's transfer to McLean, he'd treated her for a period of months then discharged her. The last anyone had heard, Sherry had moved out of state.

"Yes, Nicole Fayette came from Sipponet Village. That's one town over from where I live." She had told him about Nicole's murder and catching the killers. She omitted the part where she'd been nearly killed herself.

"Interesting," he said, tapping his index finger on the leather steering wheel. "I assumed crimes like that were found more in cities. But aberrant human nature is aberrant human nature, no matter where."

As Alonzo pulled into the hospital parking lot to let her out, he simply said, "I'll hear from you soon?"

"Yes," she assured him. "Very soon." But she was glad he hadn't asked for a specific time.

He began to drive away then stopped and opened the passenger-side window. "Most child abductions—if not for ransom—are for sex, you know. Maybe you should profile all the Level-3 offenders in the area."

"Yes, I will." However, she was quite sure Chief Carson Burke was already doing that.

"It's always the innocents," he said sadly and drove off.

Maybe by the time she got home from work today, Julia thought, they will have found Ponlok. Maybe he was really just lost. Or injured. Maybe he wasn't abducted at all.

She returned to her office in time for her appointment with Mrs. Davenport, a patient she'd been treating for paranoia. She didn't have time to read Sam's notes before meeting with her but Mrs. D. had been doing much better, although Julia didn't know whether to attribute it to the therapy or the medications.

"How are you feeling today, Esther?"

The neurasthenic woman sitting across from her answered "Fine" just a little too quickly. She was in her forties, a little taller than Julia, with black curly hair cut short around her thin face. She would have been attractive but for a large back mole that covered most of her right cheek.

"How did things go in my absence with Dr. Wu?"

"Fine." Her dark eyes darted around the room. Her hands seemed to have their own intentions and continually moved about.

"What is it you're looking for?"

"Nothing."

Julia waited. Most people couldn't sit in silence for very long in this situation. That was a basic technique of psychotherapy. And as anticipated, the woman finally said abruptly, "Is Dr. Wu Christian?"

"Why is that important?" She hadn't pegged her for a bigot. It was the first time in their many sessions that her patient had mentioned religion.

"I liked him. What about you, are you Christian?"

She tried not to show surprise and wished she had taken the time to read the transcripts. "What's bothering you, Esther?"

"You're a good person, Dr. Arnault, but if you aren't Christian, you won't be saved when it comes."

"When what comes?" She deftly avoided being drawn into Esther's questions.

"The end. Judgment Day."

Julia hadn't quite expected that. Esther's paranoia had mostly to do with her fear of other people. "And when will this happen?"

Esther looked around the room again. "Very soon now. Very soon."

She'd have to confer with Sam on this later. Her patient may need stronger medication, Julia decided.

"How do you know this?"

Esther looked at her intently. "This is known."

Julia wanted to say that she hadn't got the memo. There were patients she could talk that way to, but Mrs. Davenport was not one of them. "Can you tell me about it?" she said instead.

Esther sucked her cheeks in and out and considered it. "I'm not crazy, you know."

Really? Where did she think she was, Macy's? But Julia answered, "Did I say you were?"

"No." Esther pursed her lips. "You've been very understanding." She paused. "There are certain people in this world who are trying to protect us from Armageddon. But what if they fail? What if they fail?"

Julia listened as her patient talked on about the end of the world and the righteous remnant. By that point, she almost wished the End had come and gone as Esther attributed all the natural disasters and evil deeds in the world to the coming Apocalypse. As the hour wound down, Esther finally concluded with "I worry for Mankind, Dr. Arnault."

"Do you worry for yourself, Esther?" She was scrambling to bring this back to her patient's real concern.

The woman looked away.

"Are you afraid you're unworthy?" Julia persisted.

"It's already been determined."

Beyond that, Esther would say nothing and the hour concluded, in Julia's estimation, unsatisfactorily.

After she left, Julia began writing up her notes, but she had a difficult time posing her recommendation. For centuries, sincere religious people have believed in the Apocalypse. Who was she to say it was paranoia? But the part of "certain people" was a different twist. Esther wasn't afraid there were enemies after her but rather she was afraid the "certain people" might fail in their altruistic attempt to save the world. Trust Esther to come up with a new one. Julia felt she had let herself be blindsided because she hadn't done her homework. She hoped the rest of the day wouldn't go like this.

* * *

About six o'clock, when Adam arrived back at the bog, they still had not found Ponlok nor any sign of him. The sun was setting and the trees cast shadows over the landscape in patches. The red berries against the vines gave a claret hue to the entire bog. As he stood there, a small brown toad hopped over his boot on his journey into the dead leaves lining the road.

He found Chaya squatted on her haunches by the side of the bog, her forehead resting on her knees and her arms wrapped around her shins. She looked, he thought, like a black hole collapsing in on itself. She was in a tight little ball waiting to transform or disappear. He extended the flip-flop to Chaya.

"Is this Ponlok's?"

She looked up and gently took it from his hand and held it to her face. She neither cried nor moaned, her grief transcending sound. B.J. stood silently next to her.

Adam could almost read the boy's thoughts as B.J. stared at the green flip-flop. The day Ponlok had gone missing and B.J. came running to Adam's house, the boy had gone into the kitchen to get a glass of water and Adam found him there in the corner slumped to the floor, crying. He said he was responsible for looking out for Ponlok. He should have done a better job of it. If he had, his friend wouldn't have disappeared. Adam had tried to reassure him that it wasn't anything he did to lose Lucky. But Adam had the feeling that B.J. was crying as much for his mother as for his friend.

Maybe B.J. had the notion that when he came back today he'd be the one to find his Ponlok. He would be the one to notice a scrap of clothing or a footprint and he would be the one to lead them all to Lucky at the end of the trail. And he would be a hero. And maybe that would make everybody forget that he should have been looking out for Lucky. After all, Lucky was his friend, and younger.

Adam understood that feeling all too well. He'd been training a new sniper-recruit in 'Nam when the new guy—barely younger than himself—stepped on a land mine. Adam had instructed him to walk in his footprints. But the new guy went off the path and there was nothing Adam could do to save him, only back away. He was responsible for the kid and no amount of rationalization would dispel his guilt. He had never even called him by his name. Vincent. Panelli.

He watched as B.J. squatted down and curled himself up into the same ball of concentrated matter as Chaya.

"B.J." Adam said gently, putting a hand on his shoulder. "B.J. Time to go."

The boy just shook his head.

"It's getting dark. We have to leave."

"I don't want to."

Then Adam grabbed him firmly under his arms and pulled him out of the black hole and onto his feet. He did the same with Chaya. She came up so easily, like lifting a balloon. She let Adam lead her to the truck. B.J. followed.

All the shouting for Ponlok stopped as the sky grew dark and the searchers emerged from the woods. Adam gently took the flip-flop from Chaya and walked over to Carson Burke.

He explained where it had been found and Burke turned it over to the K-9 handlers for the search tomorrow.

"It's not a good sign," Burke confided to Adam. "It's unlikely the boy would go barefoot. Not in these woods."

After bringing B.J. home, Adam started on his way to meet Kip at Dottie's. Kip would have driven down from Boston and had his meeting with Amos by now. But impulsively, Adam decided to swerve off to Elgin Bradburn's house in what the locals called The Hollow or Pink-Eye Village but what Adam had called 'home' for most of his youth. The labyrinth of Jucket homes was a no-entry zone for most outsiders, with only one road in and out. It was a maze of back roads, dead ends, and dirt driveways leading to small one-story houses much like Tully's. Most of the homes were necklaced with junk cars, winch trucks, bucket trucks, dozers, front-end loaders, mobile log-splitters, dogs, ponies, chickens, and primary-colored plastic slides, swings, and tricycles.

Elgin Bradburn's house was tucked far back on his property with a field next door and woods behind him. He, his son Otis, and grandnephew Judd Vaughan were woodchoppers. Adam knew that Judd fought chickens too, but he hadn't been able to catch him at it. Whatever legal income they had came mostly from taking down trees, splitting wood, grinding stumps, and selling firewood. He found Elgin sitting in the dark cab of his pick-up truck in the driveway, drinking and thinking.

"Getting cold, Elgin," Adam said as he approached the truck.

"Yup," the stocky old man acknowledged without turning his head.

"You out here for your health?"

"Can't stand them screaming meemies."

Otis and his wife Cora had a new baby, conceived after the death of their young daughter, Jeannine. And Minna—Elgin's granddaughter from his daughter who'd left Pittsley and left Minna behind—had a second child too; father unspecified, although it was commonly thought to be her cousin Judd's, just like the first one.

Elgin put the whiskey bottle to his mouth and drew a deep draught. He wiped the rim with his palm and offered the bottle to Adam. Adam took a swallow. It was pure rotgut, burning down his esophagus into his stomach and leaving his mouth numb.

"Much obliged." He wiped the bottle and passed it back to Elgin.

Elgin took another hit. Then a third. He looked through the windshield as though fixed on the moon. "Don't think I can do the dive-bomb on Kalijah anymore—"

When the Saturday-night band played the song 'Kalijah' at the end of the evening at the local watering-hole and Elgin was sufficiently tanked up, he would get up on the table and dive onto his head on the last thrumming notes of the fiddle. It was a tradition that had gone on for years.

"—getting too old," he concluded.

"We're all getting old, Elgin."

Elgin turned to look at him for the first time. His eyes were bloodshot. "I remember when you was growing up. You was born over there." He pointed to another house across the way and down the road. It was painted yellow and looked like a piece off a Monopoly board. "Then your ma went to Brockton. Got married. Got you. And came back. That was a long time ago. How old are you now anyway?"

"Fifty-something," Adam answered. Fifty-four, fifty-five, he had to think about it.

"I'm seventy-five. Went to school with your momma. Wasn't your pa Polish or something?"

"Yes."

"Kept to himself. Good man?"

"Yes."

"That's good." He took another drink of the whiskey then passed it to Adam, who drank and returned it. "How come you never got married?"

"I don't know." The liquor was taking the edge off the day. It made his shoulders feel loose and tingly.

Elgin stared at the sky as though it might move on him.

"I came to ask you a personal question, Elgin. Do you mind?" Adam said.

"Depends on the question."

Inside the house, the babies wailed in stereo. Elgin closed his eyes and shook his head in disgust. Adam tried to ignore them.

"Dottie mentioned that some of the guys were talking about their land here and a letter from the town. Do you know what's going on?"

Elgin opened his eyes, but his voice did not exhibit any surprise that gossip had reached beyond the Jucket community. "Letter says they're planning on taking property."

"You get a letter like that?"

"Yep. Today. Threw it away."

"Who else got that letter?"

"I don't know exactly. Next door," he gestured to the right, "and next door," he gestured left, "down the street."

What the hell is going on? Adam thought. Tully, Amos, and now the Juckets?

Elgin passed Adam the bottle again. Adam leaned against the truck and silently took another hit.

Maxwell Kipper was of course already waiting for him at Dottie's. Adam immediately spotted the shorter man in the corner booth. He was the only one in the restaurant wearing a Brooks Brothers suit.

"You're late, asshole," Kip greeted him.

"Sorry, fartface." Adam slid in opposite him.

"Jesus, you smell like a brewery."

"Distillery," Adam corrected. "Anyway, I had to see somebody after spending the day searching for a missing kid."

"What missing kid?"

"A Cambodian boy who disappeared off Amos Hall's bog."

"Funny, I just met with Amos. He never mentioned it."

"Well, he probably had his mind elsewhere." He didn't feel like going into the whole story of Ponlok's disappearance. It didn't have anything to do with the problem at hand. "Anyway," he continued "I've found out a few other things today."

"Such as?" Kip frowned.

It made him look, Adamn thought, like a terrier on a mouse.

"Let's eat first." Adam pointed to the pink paper placemat on the pink-and-black vinyl tablecloth. The front side of the mat contained Dottie's menu in black ink with the border-lined advertisements that never changed: *Buckley Builders, Cranland Trucking, Agway Feed & Grain, Engine Block*, among others.

Over the homemade salmon loaf with bernaise sauce, Adam told Kip about the letter that Tully received. He also told him about his visit to Elgin Bradburn.

"Any idea what's behind all this?" Kip asked.

Adam took out his fountain pen, turned over the pink paper placemat from under his plate, and drew a rough map of Pittsley. "Look, here's Tully." He pointed to his friend's house, then moved his pen to the contiguous areas on the map and tapped it. "And here are the Juckets.

Let's assume for the minute that they've all gotten notices, too. I'll check that out, but I think it's a good bet. What does this look like to you?"

Kip leaned over to take it all in. "Like something major is being planned." He pointed to a strip of land between Tully and the Juckets. "What about Babe Hampley's place?"

"I don't know." All Adam knew was that after Babe had died three years ago, the foundation-house he had lived in remained empty and the property was untended.

"I'll check it out," Kip offered, studying the map.

If the town took all their properties, Adam calculated, it would combine into one hell of a large land mass to the east of Lake Tipisquin and then to the west beyond Amos Hall's bog. There would be perfect access from the route locally called The Cranberry Highway, running north to Boston and south to the Cape and intersecting with other major highways. All kinds of commercial development could go in there.

"That's a lot of land. And a lot of access," Kip said, echoing Adam's thoughts.

"Nothing gets past you, my friend."

Kip ignored him. "So the question is, what's the town going to do with that land?"

"Don't they have to have hearings and proposals to the Planning Board to make a move like this?"

Kip swiped his plate with half a buttermilk biscuit. "When's the last time you went to a Selectmen's meeting or a Planning Board meeting?"

Adam shook his head. "I don't go to those things."

"And that's how it happens." Kip put butter on the other half of his biscuit and soaked up the remaining sauce.

"But don't they have to notify the landowners before they do anything?"

"They have. They all got a letter, didn't they?"

"But there's still time to reverse this," Adam said. "Isn't there?"

"You think so?" Kip dabbed at his mouth with his pink paper napkin. "Chester still makes the best damn salmon loaf on the East Coast."

"You mean this is all a *fait accompli?*"

Kip shrugged. "At the local level anyway. We can try arguing it in a higher court, but that's already been done elsewhere. Unsuccessfully."

"Then, what?"

"First, let's find out what's being proposed. And by whom?"

"By *whom*? Since when are you adding *m*'s to your *who*'s?"

"Since I became literate, you sorry-ass hick. What do you think, I go before the Supreme Court and say 'youse judges'?"

"You've been before the Supreme Court?" Adam snickered. "On what charge?"

Kip grinned and shook his head. "One thing about you, Adam, you never fail to remind me where I came from." He looked cursorily at the menu. "I think I'll have dessert. Nobody makes lemon meringue pie like Dottie." He deliberately said that within her hegemony.

"Do you hear that Chet?" Dottie shouted. "Kip wants my pie. Loves my pie, pie, pie."

"Yeah," her husband bantered back, "wait until he finds a fingernail in it."

"Toenail," Dottie shot back to all the customers' amusement.

They all knew that although Chester made the meals, only Dottie made the desserts. Years before meeting her husband, she had had the best bakery in town. Chester came from Somerville and when they opened the restaurant together, all her clientele came for the pies and cakes but soon found they liked the meals equally as well. It began a good-natured public rivalry between chef and boulanger.

"What about you, Adam?"

"I'm full, Dottie, thanks. Just coffee."

"Come on, skinny, how about some cranberry cobbler?"

She looked so expectant that Adam relented and she left to get their orders with a satisfied nod.

"So," Adam said, "what's going on with you these days? I haven't seen you in months. How's your secretary? Or should I say 'very significant other'?"

"Terri's fine. And Julia?"

"She just became a grandmother."

"Ouch." Kip grinned. "Does that make you a proxy grandpa?"

"Stow it. Your daughter will probably be doing the same thing to you one day soon."

"Too true."

"Do you see her much?"

Kip rapped his fingers on the table. "Not much. Her mother never forgave me for the divorce."

"Wasn't she the one who wanted it?"

"She also wanted more money. You know how it goes, lawyers are sharks."

"I thought you represented yourself."

"I did. I'm the sharkiest."

"We'll see about that."

Dottie returned expertly balancing the two coffees and two desserts in her hands. Kip's face, Adam thought humorously, was absolutely beatific.

* * *

When Julia had lived in the Boston condo with Phillip, they had very expensive, very modern, very Swedish furniture with clean lines and hard surfaces. Phillip hated clutter. Julia had always felt that if anyone walked into their home there would be no clue as to the personalities of the occupants. The artwork and objets d'art were chosen by a decorator, a man Julia referred to as The Void. Everything he chose—and that Phillip liked—was almost impersonally beautiful but, to her, magazine cold.

Now Adam was the complete opposite, that is except for his clinic. His home was what Julia called Man-town. Rugged, run-down, rough, and utterly haphazard. But the one thing it was, was definably Adam.

Her own home was in-between both extremes but clearly leaning more towards random. Her furniture was large and comfortable. Her colors were bright and warm. Her artwork was whatever she liked, and for now, she liked Impressionism. She might change it in a while, and that was what she liked best. She didn't feel her home was sterile or static. It had taken a lot of work to make this old house into her own, but she had done it and was happy here. There was nothing so comforting as curling up into her overstuffed armchair at night, reading a book and listening to her favorite classical music wrapped in a large red knit shawl. She needed that serenity at the end of a stressful day. On the other hand, when she was cooking or cleaning, it was all classic rock.

Tonight, it was doo-wop on the radio as she concocted a sweet dense flan-cake from a Portuguese recipe. Cat lay on the floor with expectations of licking the bowl. The recipe called for an impossible number of eggs, eight whole and four yolks, along with sweetened condensed milk, a small amount flour and baking powder poured over caramelized syrup on the bottom of the bundt pan and baked in a water bath.

She had changed from her work clothes to jeans and a turquoise fleece top. She kept the thermostat at fifty-five but the warmth of the stove was enough to take the chill off the house, and she left the oven door open after removing the cake. By the time Adam arrived, the house was cozy, Julia had brewed a pot of decaf coffee, and the cake was sitting on the coffeetable.

"I think I'd rather have a whiskey," Adam said eyeing the coffeepot.

"Yeah," she agreed, "I'd rather a have a wine, myself."

As they sat on the soft leather sofa, they clinked glasses as though sharing the relief of a difficult day. She cut herself a very small piece of the cake and gave him a larger slice drizzled with more caramelized sugar. How could he consume six times what she could and still not gain an ounce? She couldn't even carry an extra five pounds without showing it in her stomach and butt. Sometimes she resented that he was so tall and raw-boned, but oh well, she did enjoy feeding him because he so obviously loved to eat.

"Is there any news about the Cambodian boy?" Julia asked.

"No. We had to end the search at dark."

"No sign of him at all?"

Adam shook his head. "Burke's called in the State Police and they put out an Amber Alert in case anyone spots him." He told her about Charlie and Fred and the green flip-flop. "I think the Staties will go back to search with Burke and his men again tomorrow."

"And you?" She balanced a forkful of flan-cake and slipped it into her mouth. It was so smooth and sweet. It had the texture of creamy cheesecake but tasted like a cloud of spun sugar.

"I've got clinic in the morning. I'll try to join up with them later."

"Was his mother there today?"

"Yes."

"How is she doing?" Julia asked as she took another forkful of the dessert. She was going to have a hard time with any leftovers. Maybe she should pack it up with him in the morning and get temptation out of the house.

"She seemed resigned. I don't mean accepting it, but I get a feeling that she's been through a lot and she expects bad things to happen to her. When I look in her eyes I see a familiar anguish."

Julia put down her fork. "Are you still getting flashbacks?" His memories of Vietnam had diminished, but she knew they still surfaced once in a while.

"No, not that. I've come to terms with that. But it just reminded me of how desperate life can be for some people. You probably see that in your patients."

"Sometimes." She put down her plate and stared at the remainder of the flan cake sitting there, luring her. "Sometimes they're so despairing, they make up rescuers."

He looked at her quizzically.

"Never mind. Just a patient I was thinking about."

He nodded then changed the subject. "Did you see Dr. Alonzo today?"

"Yes. We looked at his proposed offices this morning, but I didn't give him a definite answer yet."

"Why not?"

Julia shrugged. "I'm not sure I want to go into private practice."

"Why not?"

She poked him teasingly in the abdomen. "Are you going to play prosecutor with me?"

"You're evading the question."

"Yes." She leaned into him and he put his arm around her.

"Why?"

She drew back and looked into his piercing grey-green eyes. "Stop it, Adam. I'm not ready to answer, and don't ask 'why not'? I need to have my thoughts percolate for a while. And as much as I appreciate your input, I don't want to make a hasty choice." Then she felt remorse at overreacting and added flippantly, "Because if it goes sour, I'll blame you of course."

Adam chuckled. "Okay, I'll back off."

"And I'll let you know as soon as I sort it out." She settled back into the sofa. "So what did Kip have to say tonight?"

"He's representing Amos Hall in the eminent domain case."

"Amos Hall? What about Tully?"

He explained what he'd learned about all the land involved and concluded, "I don't think Kip's too optimistic about winning. The legal battle was fought and lost in Connecticut. But if there's any way to combat this, he'll find it."

"I hope so. But isn't there anything else they can do to stop this?"

"Such as?"

"I don't know. Something."

Adam finished his piece of flan-cake and cut himself another. "You know, this is really fantastic."

"Take it with you tomorrow. You can have it for lunch."

"Okay with me."

She smiled contentedly as they sat quietly for a moment. Then her expression darkened.

"Are you ever afraid that this won't last?"

He looked at her in consternation. "This, us?"

"No," she gestured with her hand. "I mean the way we live. I sometimes feel like that little chipmunk I saw yesterday. Going about his business, storing his food for winter, preparing for the cold and yet fully expecting to make it through to spring. Completely unaware that a car could back over him, or that the stone wall could crumble, or that there might not be enough nuts, or that some predator will find him—I don't know, it just seems naïve to go on as usual when so much disaster is happening in the world. And so many people dying."

His steady gaze held hers. "Do I think about it? Yes. Is there anything I can do about it? Limited."

She put her hands inside the long sleeves of her fleece top to warm them. "I worry that my grandson won't have the same privileges I've had growing up. The essential ones like heat, food, water, clean air, and a childhood without fear. Will all of that be there for him in the coming years?"

"Is it there for children in hellholes like Darfur now?"

"No," she acknowledged sadly, conjuring up the faces on television of the starving and dying African victims. "It's not very fair, is it?"

"The cosmos has no regard for what's fair."

"You don't believe in God?"

He didn't look at her. "If there is one, I don't concern myself with him and he returns the favor." He finished the last of his whiskey in one gulp. "Let's shelve this for the night. It's been a long day."

"Agreed."

He got up from the sofa but she did not move.

"Do you want me to leave?"

"No, of course not," she said immediately. She pointed to the half-empty bottle. "I think I've had a little too much wine."

"I'd say that was only two glasses."

She gradually pushed herself up and started to fall back again when he caught her and set her on feet. "Funny, that never used to bother me."

"Maybe you're just out of practice," he joked.

Or maybe, she thought with a shudder, I'm getting too old to hold my liquor.

As he took her hand and led her upstairs to the bedroom, she took a fit of giggling.

Tuesday, October 3rd

Julia lay in bed with her head on Adam's shoulder as he cradled her close to him. They were still pressed together after making love and she held him around his chest, smelling the mixed fragrances of his body and after-shave, her arm rising and falling with his breaths.

"This is the best part of the day," she murmured.

He kissed her tenderly, not in foreplay, but rather an acknowledgment that this was almost a stronger intimacy than actual lovemaking.

How would she feel, she thought, if he left her? It would be worse than the divorce from Phillip. Over the last years of their marriage, they had lost that intimacy of quiet touch, and their fighting was not the hot lusty anger of a couple's passion. They were frigid words.

"All we do is argue," she had complained to Phillip one evening.

"Then don't," he'd answered as he walked out of the room without looking at her.

She'd tried that. Tried to keep her disappointment hidden, tried to recapture the things she did when they were newlyweds, embarrassing things in embarrassing lingerie. She smiled, planned parties, filled their social calendar, and suggested vacation weekends. She did everything except argue. None of it, of course, worked. He had already left the marriage.

She dreaded the idea that she would ever have to go through that again. But Adam, she believed, would have the decency to tell her it was over. And she would survive, just as she had before.

She looked out the window at the brightening sky. Past six-thirty. Time to get up.

"I wish we could stay here for another hour. But I've got to be at work by eight."

"I know," he said. "But we have the weekend ahead of us."

She slid out of bed and slipped on her black velveteen bathrobe. He made no move to get up.

"What time are your clinic hours today?"

"Not until this afternoon."

"Loafer," she teased as she headed towards the bathroom and turned on the shower to heat up the water.

"Oh, yeah?" Within an instant, he was across the room and pinning her against the wall in an urgent embrace.

She succumbed for a minute then disengaged herself. "I've got to shower and get going," she protested.

"Are you sure?"

"Mostly sure," she laughed.

With that, he pulled her into the shower. It sprayed both of them with icy water.

"Ye-ow! Cold! Cold! Cold!" she sputtered.

He quickly turned off the tap as she grabbed a towel. "Come to think of it, I didn't hear the furnace go on this morning. But were generating our own heat," he mock-leered at her.

"Oh, no," she shook her head, "please don't tell me I need a new furnace."

"Or it could be the water heater." He took a towel and wrapped it around himself. "I'd better check it out."

They dressed quickly and he went downstairs to the cellar.

As Julia finished making scrambled eggs and toasting thick slices of sweet bread in the skillet, Adam came up from the basement with a less than optimistic look. "It's the water heater."

She should have anticipated it. It was an old house with old appliances. "How much do you think that will cost?"

"Not as much as the furnace. Three or four hundred, maybe, plus installation. That might be another one or two hundred."

There goes my Christmas trip to California, she thought. Five hundred dollars was a lot of money to her right now. It was times like these she wished she'd asked for alimony.

"Oh, well," she said, putting on her game face, "if I can get someone to do it today, at least we can play drop-the-soap in the shower tomorrow."

Adam came up behind her and kissed her on the neck.

He knows, she thought.

* * *

"When, exactly, did you notice the kid was missing?" The kid Adam was referring to was Leroy's goat. He and Leroy Bingham stood at the wooden railing overlooking the pasture.

"When I turned them in last night. That's when I left the message for you." Leroy tugged down his John Deere cap over his bald head. He wore a frayed-at-the-cuffs denim jacket over his jeans. Although he was a small wiry man, his hands were thick, worn with hard work, and his fingers were square at the tips.

The pasture was still green and lush with large shade trees in the center for the sun-sensitive white Saanens. The fall foliage was luminescent crimson, orange, and yellow with splotches of green. Here and there were piles of boulders for the goats to mount. The buck, looking alertly at them with his ears forward, stood on the highest rock pile. Beyond the back railing was one of the town cemeteries, to the far left was woods, and to the right was Leroy's farmhouse, with his vegetable garden beyond.

The front rows of corn had been cut down and plowed under although the back rows were still producing the last of the season's ears. Only green tomatoes were left on the vine and these would be picked for relish before the first frost. The zucchini and peppers were at the end of their growing, but the little potatoes left after harvesting the big ones still lay on the ground. Called 'pig potatoes,' many of the locals—including Adam and Leroy, himself—preferred them.

In the pasture, the small herd of Swiss goats were in good flesh and clear-eyed, hooves trimmed, recently shorn. They were rugged animals if kept well, which these were. Leroy had healthy well-fed animals weighing as much as a small man at about one hundred and fifty pounds—just about Leroy's weight—and he typically called Adam at any hint of a veterinary problem. They were good milk producers with high butterfat. Fresh goat cheese, so popular in the region, was as moist and mild as cream cheese, not pungent and chalky like the supermarket variety. The farmer always got a good price for his products, but more than that, Leroy loved his goats.

"Just the one goat?"

"This time. My best billy." He stuffed his hands in the pockets of his overalls and stood with his legs apart as though wanting to punch the fence but restraining himself.

"You didn't see or hear anything?"

"Nope. I give them fresh water in the morning and around Noon. They were all there, so it had to be in the afternoon sometime when me and Mary was out. She had a doctor's appointment. Not doing so good with the rheumatism."

"I'm sorry to hear that."

The last time Adam had seen Mary Bingham, rheumatoid arthritis had put her in a wheelchair. The once-petite farmer's wife had swelled up like a water ball. But her spirits were good and they had both been optimistic about the new medication she was taking. That was about three months ago. Apparently the medication hadn't been effective.

"We come home," Leroy continued. "I put her to bed. Make supper. Read the newspaper. Maybe nod off for a bit. Then I go out to put them in the barn and that's when I do a count. Just habit. And I see there's one short. I look around for a long time. Maybe he's stuck somewhere. So I look everywhere. But no. I check again this morning. No billy."

"Let me look around a little."

"Suit yourself." Leroy turned to go back into the house, then turned back. "I heard there's others missing besides mine."

"Yeah."

"What's going on?"

"I don't know yet."

"Don't make no sense."

No, it didn't, Adam agreed as he walked along the railing, intending to cut through the woods to the back end of the pasture where the stone wall separated Leroy's property from the Pittsley Cemetery.

He could see it was a wall that extended well beyond the cemetery in either direction. Very likely, the large stones in that wall came from the pasture, the results of ox and plow of generations past, giving evidence of a forgotten history. How many thousands of stone walls crisscrossed Massachusetts? He wondered what that would be in miles and tried to imagine the tons upon tons of rocks, stones, and boulders the pioneer farmers had to remove manually in order to farm the land. Not exactly the pyramids, but many of the stone walls, like Leroy's, were fit together without mortar; just rock against rock, standing no more than hip-high, but so solid, so enduring as to have withstood centuries.

He knew the native Americans had rarely used enclosures. Had no need for them. It was the colonists who created fenced-in areas, mostly to keep their livestock in or to keep other animals out. Agriculture and livestock had altered everything here. Idly, he wondered what the landscape looked like four hundred years ago before colonization. It must have been beautiful. Not that he idealized the Native Americans. He was too much of a realist for that. But what they did not do, was despoil the land. And that began him thinking again about land ownership and the disputed issue of eminent domain.

And then he remembered he was supposed to meet Kip at the town hall, so he quickly doubled back to his truck before reaching the wall and without having found anything significant.

An hour later, Adam and Kip were sitting in the office of the Board of Selectmen with Albert Carriou, the chairman. Even seated, Carriou was nearly half-again as tall and twice as wide as Kip. Carriou had been in office for fifteen years—mainly, his detractors thought, because of his bulk. Where, Adam wondered snidely, did he buy his clothes?

Kip looked every part the diminutive Boston lawyer. He was wearing a conservative lightweight grey pin-stripe wool suit with a white shirt and black leather belt and shoes. It was a look, Adam thought, that typified the profession, even down to the grey silk tie with a small black geometric pattern. It contrasted sharply with his own attire—jeans, boots, and navy sweater over a long-sleeved blue shirt, along with his usual camouflage jacket. He rarely wore anything more formal except when he took Julia out someplace nice, admittedly not often enough.

"To what do I owe the pleasure of this rare visit, gentlemen? Formal or informal?"

Kip took the lead. "I thought we might have a friendly chat, Al, and maybe we won't have to get into the legalese just yet." Kip tapped the black leather attaché case next to his chair.

"Said the woodchopper to the tree before he swung the ax," Carriou commented. "So what's up?"

"I'm representing Amos Hall on this eminent domain business."

"I see." Albert Carriou was expressionless.

"So what can you tell me about it?"

"Public information, Mr. Kipper." Carriou made a dismissive gesture with his hand. "The Parkwood Development Corporation is going to put in a multi-use project that will enhance the land and bring in jobs and revenue to the town."

"And who is the Parkwood Development Corporation?" Adam asked, noting that Carriou did not specify any of those multi-uses.

Carriou turned his attention to him. "It's a conglomerate," he answered with a somewhat patronizing tone. "They have the finances to develop the area and the property owners will be compensated accordingly."

Carriou leaned back in his oversized ergonomic chair, whereas his visitors were seated in a plain oak chair without arms or padding. It tended to discourage long visits.

"You're not telling us anything," Kip said. "What exactly is this multi-use project for?"

"The plans have been filed with the Planning Board and they're open to inspection. Go have a look. Then you'll know as much as I do."

"You know if this goes through it's going to displace a good many people," Adam said.

"And that is regrettable," Carriou answered. "But it will go through.

You can't make the proverbial omelet without breaking eggs, you know. This is something Pittsley will benefit from. Good for the tax base. Local employment. Progress, you know."

Carriou began squaring off the papers on his desk, signaling that further conversation was futile.

Adam was about to respond rudely when Kip gave him a stern look.

"Well, we thank you for your time, Al," Kip said.

"Anytime, boys."

Adam stared at Carriou, not wanting to leave, but Kip got up and stood between them.

"Give my regards to Bertha," Kip said. Behind his back, he gestured Adam to get up.

"Will do," Carriou answered absently.

Scowling, Adam followed Kip out of the office. In the hallway, he said, "What was all that nicey-nicey shit?"

"Pick your battles, Adam. You'll get nowhere fighting him."

In the foyer, Kip dialed his Boston office on his cell phone. "Terri, I need you to look into a group called the Parkwood Development Corporation. Get me a list of the board of directors and any other information you can find out. I have to check out something else here but I should be back in a couple of hours." He listened for a minute. "Oh?" he said, then paused again. "Good work. I'll see you later." He closed the phone and put it into the leather holder on the side of his belt under his jacket.

"What's up?" Adam said, sensing the Kip had learned something significant.

"Terri looked into Babe Hampley's property. Seems that it went to land court but the town didn't put it up for auction. They're holding it."

Adam looked at him meaningfully. "I guess that completes the package."

"Maybe that's how all this began. They got the land and then got the idea." Kip began walking towards another office. "Let's go see what they're hatching."

Their next stop would be the office of the Planning Board.

Adam and Kip parted after leaving the Town Hall, Kip for Boston and Adam for Tully's house.

He found his friend in his grape arbor picking the last of the Concord grapes. Despite the earlier coolness of the morning, it had warmed up and Tully was shirtless with red suspenders crossed over his chest instead of his back. Although deeply tanned, Tully had developed an old man's sagging breasts.

Tully dropped the heavy bunches into one of a row of white buckets, kicked it over to his wife, and began filling the next one. Doris pulled the grapes off the stems, and dropped them into a bucket of water. She culled the floaters and threw them into an industrial-strength, black plastic garbage bag along with the discarded stems. The good grapes she scooped up from the bottom with a slotted spoon and put them into a blue plastic tub.

Doris had purple stains on her hands, on her yellow- and pink-striped top, on her blue and green paisley shorts, her legs, her face, and her bare feet in yellow flip-flops. When Tully wasn't looking, she would pop a grape in her mouth and smile secretly.

"'Lo, Adam," she greeted him in her sing-song voice.

Adam couldn't tell Doris' age exactly, but she was much younger than Tully. She had a large moon face and smooth skin except for little wrinkles and folds around her pale lashless eyes.

Tully turned around just as she put another grape in her mouth.

"Don't be eating them grapes, dammit. You'll be squirting all night. I told you not to eat them."

Doris pouted and looked down.

"She gets the runs," he said to Adam, "but she don't listen. Then I have to hose her off."

"Are you going to make grape jelly, Doris?" asked Adam cheerily.

She shook her head.

"Cost too much to make jelly," Tully answered. "Too much sugar. Ain't good for you anyway. I'm going to make juice and freeze it for winter. Doris'll make grape pie with the skins."

Adam had tasted Doris' grape pie. It was made with grape Jell-O and the boiled grape juice, with some of the skins for texture. Tully boasted that you could turn it upside down and it wouldn't fall out of the pie pan. 'Purple ce-ment pie,' Adam once called it and Tully got mad at him.

Grapes were Tully's best crop. Although he planted rows of strawberries, tomatoes, melons, squash, corn, and other vegetables, usually the deer consumed more than he did. He'd tried everything to discourage the invaders short of putting up a fence—which, he complained, cost too much. Last year, he put a television out in the garden with an extension cord and played the night shows on the highest volume. The deer soon got used to it. Adam had joked that Tully had provided them with dinner *and* entertainment. Tully got mad.

The year before, Tully had had the idea that if he sprinkled talcum powder on the plants, the deer wouldn't touch them. But the uninvited guests thought it was a great treat and ate it like candy. Adam said…well, whatever he'd said, Tully got mad.

Everything Tully tried—this year, planting garlic between the rows—ended in defeat. He'd allowed a hunter on his land last year but the deer had outsmarted him. And so went the war between man and beast.

"I've been asking around," Adam said. "Seems like a lot more people than you got that letter about the town taking their land."

"Nobody's going to take my land." Tully continued picking grapes.

"What they'll do is offer to buy it."

"I ain't selling."

"Then they'll take it without buying it and you'll get nothing. That's what happened in other places." Adam glanced at Doris but she was impassive as though immune to thought.

"I don't care what they do. I'm not leaving," Tully shouted.

"You won't have a choice. But maybe we can do something as a group."

"Like what?" He continued picking his grapes; nothing, not even dispossession, would interfere with his task.

"That's what we have to figure out. Max Kipper's going to help."

"I can't afford no lawyer."

"It's not going to cost you anything. I just wanted to let you know we're working on it."

"I'm putting up a 'No Trespassing' sign."

Doris furrowed her brow. "Does that mean Adam can't come in?"

"It's not meant for Adam," Tully barked.

"Can Julia come in?" she asked.
"Dammit, it's not meant for friends."
"Shouldn't it say that? 'All except friends'?"
"Jesus Jones, Doris, go back to work, will you?"

Adam gazed over to Babe Hampley's land next door. The concrete-block foundation he'd lived in was abandoned. The grass, brush, and young pine trees covered the front yard in amongst large patches of goldenrod.

"What happened with Babe's property, Tully?"

Tully didn't even glance in that direction but kept his full attention on the grapes. "Town put a line on it."

"A line?"

"You know, for back taxes."

A lien, Adam deduced. "Did the town offer it to you and Doris?" Even if there'd been no will, Doris was Babe's only kin, although only a cousin."

"We got some kind of notice. But I'm not paying his taxes. I can just about pay my own."

So, that's why it had gone to land court, Adam thought. There was no point in telling Tully that whatever had been owed in real estate taxes, he could have sold the land for a hundred times more.

"I don't care what they do with it," Tully added, getting agitated. "Some yukkie can build a mansion on it. They can afford it, let them pay the taxes. Don't mean nothing to me."

Adam would have stayed a little while longer, but Tully was in such a mood that he didn't see any point in lingering.

"Save me a piece of pie, Doris," Adam said kindly.

"I will, Adam. And one for Julia, too. She likes my grape pie."

"We all do, Doris."

Adam picked up Billy on his way to Cutter's. The indignation that Billy had expressed about Tully's plight was the first time in the months following Tessa's death that his friend had shown genuine interest in anything. Maybe if he could get Billy involved in this eminent domain thing, it would give him something else to focus on. Worth a try, he thought, as they drove up to 'Liberty Nation.'

Cutter's land was still gated, but not chained and locked or patrolled as it was when he was fighting the town over his secession from the Commonwealth. The sign on the gate had been expanded to include 'Wampanoag Territory.'

"I still think it's a miracle Cutter got away with making this a reservation," Billy commented as they drove up the dirt road. It occurred to Adam that he might be the only friend that Billy had who took him for rides, and he vowed to do it more often.

"I know," Adam agreed. "He was lucky nobody wanted to challenge him. Too sensitive, I guess. At least political correctness has one upside to it."

"Too bad Tully doesn't have any Wampanoag ancestors."

"I doubt that would work a second time."

"So what's the plan, Adam?"

Adam shook his head. Then, reminding himself that Billy couldn't see, he said, "Don't have one yet."

As they came to the clearing, Adam realized that Cutter's reservation was more and more looking like a colonial New England village. What had started out as one man's tax revolt, joined by his brother and their families, then other friends, neighbors, and a scattering of full-blooded Wampanoags, was now a complete community. Cutter ran the sawmill and farm with some of the other men. His wife, Angel, along with her older children had established a general store that included a bakery. Some other small collective businesses had grown up—a mechanics' garage and a blacksmith shop. They still had to go off-site for medical and dental needs and some other goods and services—like hair dye, Adam smiled wickedly thinking of Cutter's beard—but they home-schooled the children and the classroom had been expanded.

They found Cutter in the mill running lumber through the enormous saw blade. The smell of raw pine, cedar, and red oak filled the air. The shavings flew in an arc from the spinning blade onto the floor in mounds. They would use the cedar and oak sawdust for footing in the barns, and the pine for insulation in their ice house. Stacks of boards were drying in the back of the mill. They would use what they needed and sell or barter the rest. There were enough trees on the property to thin out in a forestry management program that Cutter devised. At some point, they might have to venture outside the rez for wood, but not for many years to come.

There was no possibility of conversation over the grinding and whirring noise of the sawblade so Adam gestured that he wanted to talk. Cutter removed his protective eyewear and passed off the lumber to the stocky Wampanoag man in jeans, boots, and a long-sleeved flannel shirt next to him.

As they walked back to Cutter's cabin with his German Shepherd, Hercules, at his heels, Adam was glad to see more than a sprinkling of other Wampanoags around. He didn't know what the financial arrangement was with the tribe, but evidently it was agreeable to all.

Billy and Adam settled in at the Formica table in the small kitchen in Cutter's cabin. There was no electricity in the village other than what they generated. They did have cellphones—after all, Cutter said, they weren't Amish—but they cooked mainly on woodstoves and ran their engines on kerosene and gas that, along with some other needed supplies, had to be obtained outside. They sold lumber, produce, homemade goods and crafts, and sometimes their skills in order to buy what they wanted. Other necessities were bartered with their moonshine. All in all, it seemed to be working…and that was astonishing.

"So what's doing?" Cutter asked as he put the percolator on top of the woodstove to heat up coffee.

"Remember what Tully was telling us on Sunday about his land being seized?" Adam said.

"Yeah. It's been bothering me. We're oil and water, him and me, but that don't make him less of a friend. What's he going to do?"

"He doesn't know. And the problem is, it's more than just Tully's land," Adam said.

"Who else?"

"Amos Hall. And Elgin told me he thinks some of the Juckets got the notice."

Cutter turned around abruptly. "Them fuckers." There was no doubt he meant the government.

"Amos hired Max Kipper to represent him," Adam explained. "He thought it was only his land. Just like Tully. But now we think it might be the whole parcel."

"There's got to be about five hundred acres or more," Billy calculated, "on either side of the lake."

"Holy shit. What's going on?" Cutter said.

"Not sure yet." There was still some more digging to do before Adam was ready to say. "But meanwhile, I think we need to find out exactly who got that letter."

"So how do we do this?" Cutter asked.

Adam told them they were going to canvass every one of the Juckets. His plan was to split up the houses with Cutter and Billy taking one half and Goody and him taking the other.

"But they know you, Adam, your mother was a Jucket," Billy said without a hint of disparagement. "Maybe they won't trust Cutter and me."

"They'll trust Cutter," Adam said. "And your job is to make sure he doesn't start a riot."

Cutter screwed up his face. "I'll do more than that if I have to."

"That's what I'm afraid of," Adam replied.

"And if they all got the letters," Cutter asked, "then what?"

"Then we're going to need Kip to represent all of them. Maybe some kind of class action suit."

"That ain't going to work," Cutter said. "You can't unbreak an egg. By the time it gets to court, whatever they're doing will already be done. We got to do something else."

"Like what?" asked Billy.

"Something to make them reconsider," Cutter replied. "Like I said, I've been thinking on it and," his eyes took on the look of a predator in sight of his prey, "I have an idea."

* * *

Julia sat in Sam's office for their routinely scheduled conference every Tuesday and Thursday mornings. She hadn't seen him since she'd come back to work yesterday and she was anxious to talk with him about Esther Davenport. She had read his notes—unfortunately not until after her session with the patient.

"She was improving before I left," Julia explained, "but I can't think this regression is related to therapist transition. She says she likes you."

Dr. Shing Wu removed his round wire-rimmed glasses and set them on the desk. He massaged the bridge of his nose. "I think it's unrelated to either of us, personally or professionally. But you're right, she does seem to have regressed despite her medication."

"You described her as increasingly delusional. I'm not sure I agree"

"What do you think it is?"

Julia raised her eyebrows as if reluctant to put a name to it. "Adventist beliefs have an historic religious basis. I'm not inclined necessarily to label them delusional."

Sam signed deeply. "Yes. That may be my bias. It's sometimes difficult for me when I have patients with that ideation."

"Are you a Buddhist, Sam?" She had never actually considered his personal beliefs.

He shook his head. "I grew up with a combination of Confucius and Taoism."

Julia tried vainly to recall her 'Major Religions of the World' course in college but it was so long ago. While she was familiar with the names, the concepts eluded her.

"They're more of an ethic of behavior," Sam said coming to her aid, "than a religion. Neither of which are encumbered with 'end of days' theology, or God and Satan. But as for Mrs. Davenport, I don't see this as the major problem. It's her fixation with these people she claims are trying to save the world. Maybe she's seen too many movies in this genre—demons and angels and such."

"The odd thing," Julia mused aloud, "is that she doesn't seem concerned for herself or even her family. I think she feels it's predestined. But if that's the case, I don't understand how she thinks these people of hers can alter what has been predetermined."

Sam studied her. "I don't think we should get caught up in her logic. Even if she professes not to be concerned for herself, she's displaying a lot of anxiety about it. That's where we need to start."

He was right, as usual. That was one of the things she could always depend on from Sam; he usually managed to help her strip away the layers and get to the heart of things. Although he was still her boss, Sam had long since become a friend. They'd had a brief falling out when Sam didn't oppose the Superintendent when that hack removed Julia from a case—involving her patient, Cheryl Fayette—because Julia was stirring up the twenty-year-old murder of Sherry's mother. But then Sam went against protocol and made the connection between Julia and Sherry's new psychiatrist at McLean's, who just happened to be Dr. Raymond Alonzo.

"By the way," he said, "I understand you met with Alonzo yesterday."

It was if he were reading her mind, although she wasn't entirely surprised. He and Alonzo were good friends. She did wonder, though, what Alonzo had told him.

"Yes," she answered. "He did the dog-and-pony show but I haven't made up my mind yet. Any suggestions?"

"It's completely up to you, Julia," Sam said.

"I know it's ultimately up to me," she said, "but I value your advice."

"You know psychiatrists never give advice," he said dryly.

"Like you didn't advise me to get out of teaching and into clinical psychology?" she reminded him.

"Did I do that? Well, I only tell you what you already know."

"Which is, in this case?"

"Which is," he leaned back and folded his arms over his chest, "that you like and respect Alonzo, but you don't want to go in to private practice. If you did, you would have jumped at his offer."

Julia shook her head. "I'm not impulsive. You know that. I'm more the look-before-you-leap type."

"Umm-hmm."

Was that a smirk? she wondered. "What 'umm-hmm'?" she demanded. "You don't think so?"

When he didn't immediately reply, she frowned. She got the distinct feeling she was in analysis.

Finally he answered, "Why do you suppose you can't make up your mind?"

"I didn't say 'can't.'" Was she sounding like a patient? "Maybe I just want to stay here and do what I'm doing because I like it."

"And you think that's the reason?"

"Yes," Julia said with conviction, then added, "isn't it?"

Sam got up and walked around to the front of his desk and sat on the top, with one foot on the floor and the other dangling.

"Alonzo mentioned that you told him yesterday about a missing young boy in the cranberry bog?"

She nodded, wondering where he was going with this.

"Has he been found?"

"Not that I know of." She paused then said, "I have an ominous feeling it might be the same kind of abduction as all the young girls who disappeared. No one else sees a connection because Ponlok is a boy, so maybe I'm wrong."

She was comfortable saying this to Sam because she had gone to him when she was trying to figure out who killed Jeannine Bradburn, and again when she found out Sherry's mother had been murdered. He knew almost as much about those occurrences as she did.

"Perhaps not," Sam said. "What did he look like?"

"Why?"

He simply looked at her and did not answer.

She shrugged. "I've seen the flyer with his photo, but it's not very telling. He looks," she scrambled for the word, "sweet. Now will you tell me why?"

"Just that some young Asian males, particularly if undernourished, can seem almost feminine in appearance. This is something I know a little about—because I'm Asian and I was particularly thin and underdeveloped as a youth."

Julia tried to recall more about the flyer Adam had showed her. "He does seem small and thin, but it's hard to tell."

Sam nodded. "Let's make the assumption, at least for our purposes, that the boy was malnourished. That he may have had traditional long hair. May have dressed androgynously."

Julia immediately grasped what he was suggesting. "You mean they thought they were abducting a girl?" Then came the fearsome thought: What would they do when they discovered their mistake? Obviously, they didn't let him go.

"Perhaps I should talk to his mother," she said. "Do a little investigating."

"And that's what you should do."

She nodded.

"I said," Sam reiterated emphatically, "that's what you should do."

Didn't he just say that? It wasn't like Sam to be redundant.

"I...will."

Sam shook his head and rolled his eyes. "I mean you should consider investigative psychology. Your instincts are good and that's obviously what interests you the most. And that's probably why you can't make up your mind to go with Alonzo. Even he felt you were more animated in talking about this than you were about his offer."

Julia felt the cliché of her mouth dropping open.

Sam went on. "I have some connections in the police department."

Julia was still feeling a little speechless but managed to say, "I'm not qualified."

"It would mean taking more courses. But that shouldn't daunt you. You're still young enough to change direction. And you're a strong woman, Julia, don't underestimate yourself."

She didn't feel strong. She didn't know if she could go through another transition. She had gone into a deep depression after the divorce and it took all her resources to pull herself out of it and start over again.

"So, after work," he continued, "you should go talk to the boy's mother."

"Right." She got up from the chair and walked towards the door, then stopped and turned back to Sam.

He made a brushing-away gesture with his hand. Julia left his office feeling that shock of recognition that maybe Sam was right. It was there from the beginning and she never realized it. She'd done her Ph.D. dissertation on serial killers. She had been involved in two murder investigations. She didn't exactly solve the crimes but she tried to, and what she liked best was the research and investigation. 'Investigative psychology.' It sounded fascinating. But what exactly would that involve?

She would have time to find out later. Right now she needed to see her patients. But first she would have to call the plumber Adam recommended. The mundane always triumphs.

After the last of her patients, she made a phone call to Carson Burke to get the name and address of Ponlok's mother, but was told the Police Chief was out with his men still searching for the missing boy.

She had arranged to meet the plumber at her house at five o'clock. She arrived there only seconds before he did. He got out of the truck with a somewhat younger man—Mr. Rezendes being in his seventies and introducing his fifty-year old son as his "boy" who was going help him lift the water heater out of the truck and down the stairs.

"You're Dr. Sabeski's friend," he said as he worked.

She smiled shyly and nodded. She knew Adam had called him first to let him know she would be contacting him.

"Doctor Ski is a good man."

She nodded again.

"When things were tough with me ten, twelve years ago, he fixed up my dog for free. Operation, medication, everything."

"Yes, that's the way he is," she said. And that's why he was no better off financially than she was. But it's one of the things she loved about him.

"Good man, Doctor Ski," he pronounced as he and his silent son hefted the water heater onto a two-wheeler.

After Julia let them in, she explained she had to leave and would he please put the bill on the kitchen table?

She decided to take Cat with her to Amos Hall's bog. Julia usually took her dog to work, but the past two days she'd been too busy. So as soon as Julia said "ride," the dog became so excited she had to pee and then jumped in the car with a visible grin.

If only life were so dog-easy, Julia thought as she gave Cat a hug and started her car.

As Julia drove up the long dirt road to the bog, she saw the cruisers, including the State Police, parked alongside the holding pond. Cat reacted to the dogs barking in the distance merely by a cock of her head. Julia heard men's voices calling out the name, "Ponluck Nim." In between, she detected a younger man's voice yelling "Lucky!" It had to be Billy's son, B.J. He must have come here right after school. And wasn't that Pastor Ryman's car amongst the cruisers? Martin must be helping in the search, too. That would be just like him, she thought.

She caught up with Burke and one other officer near the far end of the bog.

"Chief Burke," she greeted him, "any sign of the boy?"

"Hi, Julia. No, not yet." He automatically swatted away the insects. "What's up?"

"I was hoping to speak with his mother. Is she here?"

"No, she had to go back to work."

"Oh," said Julia disappointed. "Do you know where?"

"She'd be home by now." Burke pulled out his notebook. "Chaya Nim." He flipped through a couple of pages. "She's with the rest of the Cambodian group at a house on 2157 Third Street in Fall River. That's down by Kennedy Park, near the water."

"What do you think happened to the boy, Chief?" Julia asked as she wrote down the information in her own notebook, determined to see the woman right away.

Burke shook his head. "We've done a pretty thorough search and the dogs haven't picked up a trail even with a shoe. Not exactly a shoe—"

"A flip-flop?" Adam had told her about his find.

"Yes. The dogs followed the scent in but it disappeared. I don't know how, but I don't think he's still in there."

"Could he have been abducted?"

"It's possible. I don't know what else to think. If he was dead or injured we would have found him by now. Burke gazed past her into the woods and expelled his breath. His expression seemed to say, 'Not again.'

"I'll talk to his mother."

He nodded and she left him there still staring off into the woods as though the boy might miraculously materialize. She got back into her car and headed south on Route 24 towards Fall River.

The apartment was on the third floor of a three-story brownstone house that looked old and burdened by the weight of so many tenants.

The first thing Julia encountered as she climbed the worn wooden stairs in the entryway was the smell of aromatic food. The spices enveloped her. She hadn't eaten since breakfast and suddenly she was famished. The stairs creaked as she went up and she held tightly onto the banister that had been stripped of its varnish by use.

The second thing Julia noticed coming from behind the closed doors was the sound of foreign languages. Not a clamor but more like the orchestral background to a movie scene where something else of interest was happening.

On the first floor, she was certain she was hearing Portuguese. Probably Brazilian Portuguese, she decided. The immigrants from Portugal would likely live in the already established communities in New Bedford and the surrounding areas. They wouldn't necessarily mix with the Brazilian Portuguese who were more recent arrivals.

On the second floor, she recognized the voices speaking Spanish. Possibly Guatemalans.

On the third floor, came soft musical voices in an Asian language she couldn't decipher and assumed it was Cambodian. The smell of their food made her envision sizzling slices of marinated meat in peanut sauce with coriander and hot peppers. In her mind, she imagined families going about the business of making supper and quietly talking about the day's activities.

The actual scene when a young Cambodian woman opened the door to the third-floor apartment, however, was less picturesque. There appeared to be only one large room with a bathroom to the left and a kitchen area near the window. Along the walls were small one-drawer cabinets, one for each tenant, Julia assumed. She was beginning to suspect that the entire house was probably full of illegals.

There were, as best as Julia could count, fifteen or sixteen mats on the floor. There were women of various ages and their children—girls of all ages but only very young boys. There were no infants or toddlers and no adolescent males. She assumed that boys of a certain age moved into the men's quarters. They all wore black pants and white blouses.

The women were sitting on their mats, eating out of simple bowls with white plastic spoons. One older woman was at the stove cooking. As she entered, they stopped eating and looked at her.

"Chaya Nim?" she said again to the woman who answered the door in bare feet.

The pretty young woman swept her hand to the left and gestured to another woman sitting on a mat in the corner. She was not eating. She sat very still, like a butterfly on a petal, Julia thought.

"Mrs. Nim?" Julia said as she approached her. "I'm Dr. Arnault. I've come to ask you some questions about your son."

Chaya Nim looked up at her as though, Julia thought, this American had come to tell her something she did not want to hear. Julia quickly asked the young woman, who spoke some English, to act as interpreter and tell Mrs. Nim that she was just here for information. At that, the seated woman inclined her head 'yes' in a way that seemed, to Julia, very regal. After the introductions, she sat down on the floor opposite Chaya.

With little prompting, Ponlok's mother produced her photograph that Chief Burke had returned to her after making copies. Mother and son stood together on the dock upon arriving in America. As Julia glanced around, she was aware many of the small dressers had similar pictures in little frames on top. Someone must have taken these photos when they arrived and no doubt charged them for it. Ponlok's smile was wide and joyful; his mother's was less of joy than apprehension.

"Does he still have long hair?" Julia asked. In the picture, his hair appeared to be halfway down his back, gathered at the nape of his neck.

"No," Chaya told the interpreter, whose name Julia learned was Veata.

"So his hair was short?" she asked Veata.

"Mrs. Nim cut hair when they come here. Hair only this long now." Veata tapped her shoulder with her finger.

"Here?" Julia patted her own shoulder to confirm.

Veata nodded.

Long enough, Julia thought, to look like a girl from the back. Mother and son were both the same height and build and they wore similarly loose clothing. They differed more in age than anything else. Yes, Julia thought, he might indeed have been mistaken for a young girl if one didn't know better. But if his abductors were hoping for a girl, what would they do with him once they discovered their mistake?

***

It was a little after five o'clock when Adam picked up Goody from the old recluse's cabin. Goody was ensconced back home after briefly living on Cutter's reservation. He lived with Cutter for only two weeks after his discharge from the hospital when he'd had his initial bout with diabetes. He was too independent, he said, even for Cutter's independence, and he had retreated to his shack in Pittsley Woods.

"Why are we going to see them people?" Goody asked after Adam told him to come along while he interviewed the Juckets. Amos was a Swamp Yankee like Cutter and didn't consider himself in the same category as a Jucket even if Adam was.

"To find out if they got the eminent domain letters, too."

"What do you need me for?" the old man growled.

"Just want to air you out," Adam replied truthfully. He had been looking after Goody for years, ever since his father, who'd been Goody's only friend, had died.

"What a pain in the ass you are, boy."

"Yup."

Adam kept a three-legged stool in the bed of his truck to help Goody get in and out of the cab, even though his arthritis was doing a little better now since he was taking an anti-inflammatory. Goody hated having to take medicine and that, along with his diabetes injections, made him crankier than usual.

As they drove over the cart path from Goody's shack onto the tar road, Adam asked, "Do you know anything about some calves and goats gone missing, Goody?"

"Heard about it."

Goody's 'intelligence' never failed to astonish him. Goody always used to prowl the woods around his shack, but he was slowly losing his mobility. How did the old man hear about anything at all, being as isolated as he was? Adam knew better than to ask.

"You hear who's doing it?"

"Nope."

Now that was surprising. If Goody didn't know, it was a very well-kept secret.

"Got any ideas?"

"It ain't for barbecue."

"Didn't think so. Re-sale?"

"I'd of heard."

Adam had had a long day at the clinic. Sometimes, like yesterday, he might only have one patient. But today the waiting room had been filled from opening to closing. He rubbed the back of his neck with his left hand while he drove. He was tired and shook his shoulders to dispel it. "So, if it's not for eating and not for re-sale, then it must be for breeding."

"Maybe," Goodie replied ambiguously.

"But who would steal animals for breeding stock when they could just buy them?"

"Them that can't afford them," Goody said as if it were obvious.

That was a possibility, Adam conceded. In any event, whoever had the animals would have to keep them somewhere. If he couldn't figure out the 'who,' maybe he at least could find out the 'where.' He would have to do some nosing around.

As they turned onto the road leading into the midst of The Hollow, there were trucks and cars lined up and down both sides like a gauntlet.

"What's all that about?" Goody asked.

"I have no idea."

As they got closer, Adam saw a crowd of fifty or more people, formed in a ring in the field alongside Elgin Bradburn's house. As Adam pulled onto the edge of the field and parked, he heard shouting and catcalls, people yelling out bets and cheering.

"Cockfight?" Goody asked.

"No," Adam replied. "Not out in the open." Not even Judd Vaughan would risk jail for an illegal cockfight. "You stay here until I see what's going on."

Adam knew most of the people and moving through the crowd, heads turned briefly to check him out, then turned back to the action. Adam spotted old Elgin on the sidelines, along with his son Otis and his granddaughter Minna in front. Minna was jumping up and down, yelling.

"Go, Judd, go!"

Adam made his way toward the center of the circle where two men were locked in battle. Judd Vaughan was one of them. He recognized the other man as Chickie Womard, Adam's second or third cousin. Both fighters were evenly matched in weight and age, both lightweights in their early thirties. They wore their work clothes including t-shirts and boots, which suggested to Adam that the fight had been spontaneous. There was no telling how long it had been going on, but Judd seemed to be getting the worst of it. His face looked battered and his jaw seemed out of line. Chickie had a bruise on his cheek but nothing more.

The two men continued to grapple, pushing each other around the center of the makeshift ring. Finally, they shoved each other apart. Judd tried a roundhouse on his opponent and missed, which set him off balance. Chickie closed in and landed a blow squarely on Judd's nose. Judd dropped to his knees. Chickie was immediately on top of him. With his arm around Judd's throat, he knocked his opponent to the ground and threw his leg over him to prevent Judd from getting up. As Chickie squeezed the air out of him, Judd spread out his hand and weakly tapped the ground. With that signal of surrender, Chickie let go. The victor stood up and pranced around the ring of onlookers with his arms raised like Rocky Balboa.

As Judd lay on the ground, Minna rushed over to help him. He angrily shoved her away and managed to get back up onto one knee. He forced himelf to stand upright by sheer will. His nose was clearly broken and he was holding his side as though his ribs hurt. Chickie, looking relatively unharmed, retreated to the edge of the ring.

The men and women in the crowd exchanged money, having won or lost their bets, and began walking back to their vehicles.

"What was all that about, Arty?" Adam asked the young man passing by.

Arty, nicknamed Arty-the-one-man-party because he was always up for a good time, said, "Judd was making the moves on Chickie's girl, Vikki."

Adam scanned the crowd. "I don't see her here."

"Nah, they broke up a couple of months ago."

Adam nodded. That was just the way it was with them. As he turned to leave, an idea struck him. He stepped into the middle of the dispersing crowd.

"Hold on, everybody! I've got something important to tell you. This is about a letter you received from the town. Goody and I are going to come by your house to talk to some of you this evening, and Cutter Briggs and my friend, Billy Jensen, will be by to see the rest of you. Make sure everybody gets the news that we're coming. We're going to call a meeting."

There were nods and "Okay, Adam" in response as the group dispersed.

As Adam got back into the cab, Goody said, "I heard that. What's this meeting you're telling them about?"

"Tomorrow night at the Legion hall. With Max Kipper."

"Does Kip know he's going to have a meeting?"

"Not yet."

They waited in the truck as everyone left and within a few minutes, at exactly six o'clock, Cutter and Billy arrived at Elgin's field. Adam had prepared a makeshift map of the houses and divided it up between their two teams.

"We'll meet back at my house afterwards," Adam said as they each walked up to the first house assigned them.

Three hours later, Adam had visited everyone on his half of the map, and everyone they talked to had received the same letter. And everyone declared his intention of coming to the meeting.

Goody had petered out after an hour-and-half and waited at Elgin's for Adam to finish. On the way home, Adam told him he was going to pick up pizzas and beer, giving his old friend a legitimate excuse to go home on account of his diabetes rather than admit he was tired.

When Adam arrived back at his house, Cutter and Billy weren't there yet so he phoned Amos Hall to inform him about the following night's meeting. Amos asked Adam to call the rest of the bog men since he, Amos, just couldn't face all that talking on the telephone. So Adam started with Fiona Hathaway.

She told him she'd spent the last half-hour soaking her feet in hot water and dozing on and off. It had been a long day on the bogs and she ached all over. Two of the crew failed to come, so she'd taken their place on the agitator and in corralling the berries into the vacuum truck. She was taking a chance on an early harvest but not taking a chance on the market; her berries would go directly to juice. It paid less, by ten dollars a barrel, than dry-picking and selling the whole berries to the conglomerate, but it was certain money. Her husband wouldn't have approved, but if he'd had a life insurance policy or a savings account, she might not have to worry about these things.

Adam let her finish her lament, then asked, "Can you come to a meeting tomorrow night at the American Legion Hall? Amos' lawyer has something to tell us."

Fiona agreed without hesitation.

That was when Adam realized he hadn't told Kip to be there. He immediately dialed the Boston number.

A few minutes after he arm-twisted Kipper and made the rest of his calls, Billy and Cutter showed up, tired and hungry. They collapsed into the armchairs and reported success before diving into the pizzas.

"It's a good thing Kip agreed to the meeting tomorrow night since we've already told everybody to be there," Adam said as put his feet up on the spool table.

"You didn't ask him first?" Billy said aghast.

Adam shrugged then caught himself. "I took advantage of an opportunity."

"Did you book the hall?" Billy followed-up.

"Forgot about that," Adam admitted. "But it's a weeknight. There won't be any functions."

"So what's Kip think about all this?" Cutter asked on his third slice of pizza and his second bottle of beer.

"He's still trying to track down all the company's officers, but apparently Parkwood is a holding company of some other company, which is a holding company of another company, which is a consortium—and from there, it gets pretty tangled. It will take more time to get to the actual people involved."

"You mean the town doesn't know?" asked Billy.

"The town is dealing with Parkwood's lawyers and the Planning Board is dealing with the engineers. Nobody knows the principals. Or at least nobody's saying."

"Can they do that?" Billy finished his beer and reached for another slice of pizza, moving his fingers along the edge of the cardboard box until he found one.

"What the hell do they care? It's all about the dollar," Cutter said.

"Maybe we'll know more by tomorrow night," Adam added. "All the bog owners are coming. I'll make sure Tully comes too."

"That'll be a first," Cutter cackled. "Bog men and Juckets in one room."

"And that may be the problem with your idea." Billy said.

"Nah. They'll work together," Cutter replied authoritatively. "Common cause. 'The enemy of my enemy is my friend.'"

* * *

On her way back from Fall River, after deliberating in a one-way conversation with Cat, Julia made up her mind to take a slight detour to the little Congregational Church in Sipponet Village.

The church looked like a typical New England postcard with its white clapboards and single spire over the entry door. To the left was the parsonage, a small cottage surrounded by rhododendrons and rose bushes, now past blooming. To the right was a tall black walnut tree about thirty feet high with a dome of healthy leaves from standing alone in the sunlight. There were still walnuts on the branches but many of the nuts had dropped to the ground, looking like green tennis balls amidst the grass. They gave off a citrus fragrance but handling them, she knew, would turn your fingers brown from the tannin. Only the squirrels harvested them, the nuts having such a hard shell that one would have to crack them in a vice.

In front of the church, the free-standing, glassed-in sermon board announced the week's message: *"Want an extreme makeover? Try a faith lift."* Last week, it was: *"Under same management—for over 2,000 years."* And the week before: *"No one is too bad to enter, no one is too good to stay away."* Parishioners would sometimes attend services in proportion to how much they liked the billboard ad. *"Aspire to inspire before you expire"* brought in several new faces last month.

Cat was still sound asleep in the passenger seat. She briefly thought of waking the dog to go in with her, but she seemed so content that Julia decided not to. She hated to see Cat slowing down, getting old, but at least she was still healthy. She couldn't resist stroking her soft fur, hoping the dog would feel the comfort of her hand in her sleep.

She had always had a companion dog, ever since she could remember, except during her Phillip years. Her first pet, Prince, was a terrier. She still had a photo of herself, at age five, holding Princie in a blanket. After Prince came Rusty—a mongrel rogue—and after him, sweet little Beauty. She got Cat after Karen left for New York and when Phillip began spending long evenings at work, hah. First, he didn't like the idea of having a shedding dog in their spotless condo; then he tried to win Cat over to him. But Cat was too smart to be fooled; smarter, it turned out, than Julia when it came to Phillip.

As soon as she entered Martin's office, Julia was second-guessing her impulse to talk with the Reverend Ryman. He politely invited her to sit down but did not seem to express any particular pleasure at seeing her.

"I noticed your car at Amos Hall's bog this afternoon," Julia began, sitting opposite him.

Martin nodded without saying anything.

In the desk light, his face looked particularly lined and tired. He seemed to have aged in the few months she hadn't seen him. Had she avoided him, or had he avoided her? Maybe both. Neither of them, she supposed, wanted this to be anything more than a professional visit. They had dated briefly during the time she and Adam had separated and she felt guilty about having disappointed Martin when she decided that it was Adam she really wanted to be with.

"Ponlok hasn't been found yet," she explained regarding the reason for her visit. "I think this is more than a lost child."

He nodded again.

"Martin, are we going to talk or are you just going to sit there and nod?" Julia snapped.

He folded his hands on his desk. "I'm not sure what you want me to say. I don't know any more than you do. In fact, I don't know anything about anything any more."

She recognized that defeated look; she'd seen it on countless patients. "What's wrong, Martin?"

He glanced up at the ceiling and involuntarily sighed. "After twenty-five years as a minister, seven years here in this parish, this morning I had to make a hospital visit I'd always hoped would never happen." He lowered his head. "A four-year old child, Emily Chapman, is in a coma. She's on total life support and her mother asked me to pray for her brain-damaged daughter. Oscar Chapman, Emily's step-father, is in jail, convicted of sexually and physically abusing the child to the point of near death."

"I'm so sorry," Julia said softly.

He raised his head and focused on the photo of his dead wife and three young children in front of him. They had been killed in a small-airplane crash eight years ago.

"After my family died, I went through a kind of meltdown. But in the end, I put my trust in God. I believed there was a reason for their deaths, even though I might not be able to fathom it. But what possible reason could there be for the torture and suffering of an innocent child like Emily? I can't find any." He took a deep breath and stared at her. "I'm talking to you like a shrink, I apologize."

"It's all right, it's what I do." Julia sat very still and spoke soothingly. She had never seen Martin like this. It was depression, yes, but more than that. Knowing him as she did, she was afraid he was on a theological precipice and the last thing she wanted to do was see him tumble off.

Martin shook his head like a dog shaking off water. "What did you want to ask me about the boy?"

Julia took his cue and returned to the purpose of her visit, to tap into Martin's expertise in religious cults. "Walk me through this. What if Ponlok Nim were abducted by the same cult that killed the little girls in Pittsley County?"

He blinked. "Why would you think that?"

"He might have been a mistake." She proceeded to tell him about Sam's remarks and Chaya's photograph. As he listened, she could see him processing the information.

Finally he said, "If it was a mistake——." He left the sentence hanging.

"He might already be dead. I know," said Julia. "But we still need to look for him."

"Yes, but I don't know how *I* can help. The woods have been thoroughly searched."

"I suppose if it's not a cult, there's no way you can help. Only the police can." She got up and began pacing. "But what if it is a cult? Let's assume it is. I know you know about cults. What can you tell me about them?" If anyone could explain this, she believed, he could. He even taught a course on the subject.

Martin opened his arms in a wide gesture. "There's so much."

"Okay." She turned to face him from the far side of the room. "Let's work on the assumption that this cult is local. All the dead girls were from this area, so that's a reasonable assumption. But why girls? Because they're likely to be virgins? Is it a sex cult?"

Averting his eyes, Martin replied, "It's possible. But sex cults don't generally use robes and altars."

Julia immediately thought about the Jeannine Bradburn case. "Which is what they'd found in Floyd Mather's basement. Thirteen white robes and a stone altar."

"Not to be graphic," Martin said, "but one generally finds…devices. Sadomasochistic instruments. And, frequently there are video tapes or photos."

Julia circled back to her chair and leaned on the back, looking at Martin. "If it's not a sex cult, then what? All the girls were killed and mutilated. Is it some kind of Satanic cult?"

"Perhaps."

"Come on, Martin, work with me. So the girls would be what? Sacrifices?"

Martin paused before speaking. "That's what I'm thinking."

Julia ran her hand through her hair. "You don't seem shocked, Martin. Why aren't you shocked?"

Martin cast his eyes down and spread his hands out on his desk. "I told you when we first met, there is such a thing as Evil."

"I believe what you said," Julia corrected, "was: 'If you believe in God, why not the Devil?' Or reasonably close to that."

"It comes to the same thing."

Julia sat back down in her chair and rested her elbows on the arms. She crossed her legs and studied the sharp crease in her woolen slacks. These were all delaying techniques she used to allow her mind to contend with difficult information. Finally she said, "All right, let's suppose it is a Satanic cult. What would the ritual be?"

"I don't know. There are so many."

"What about a time or a place?"

He shrugged and raised his hand in a gesture of helplessness.

"Martin, we've got to figure this out. Think. Would there likely be any particular time or place for the ritual?" He hesitated and she raised her voice and spoke slowly as though to a patient. "What comes to your mind? Let's start with that."

"I don't know about a place." Martin looked at his desk calendar. "But possibly a time."

"A time?"

"No, I mean a date. Like Halloween, on the 31st. That was originally Celtic you know. November 1st was the beginning of their New Year. And the night before, they celebrated the festival of the Lord of the Dead, Samhain. Then the Romans took the holiday over after the invasion and made it more of a party. That's actually where the bobbing for apples came in, and drinking cider…probably fermented. Then in 835 A.D., Pope Gregory made it a day of celebration for Catholic martyrs, so October 31st became All Hallows Eve, or holy evening and November 1st became All Souls Day."

Julia looked at him blankly. "That's too long."

"Sorry. It's part of the course I teach."

"No, I mean it's too far away. That's three and a-half weeks from now. Too long. They'd have to keep him too long. It's got to be something closer."

"Oh." He then looked at the calendar again. "Well, Yom Kippur is already past, although there's the Jewish holiday of Succoth on the 7th. But that's a celebration of God's benevolence in providing for the Israelites during their forty years' exodus through the desert."

Julia shook her head. "What else?"

"The Hindu holiday, Diwali, the Festival of Lights on the 21st."

Julia shook her head again.

"Columbus Day is the 9th, and October is Clergy Appreciation Month."

"Naturally," she smiled, then scowled. "It's none of those. Something else." She studied his calendar. A box at the bottom of the page caught her attention. "There's a full moon on the 7th. The Hunter's Moon. This Saturday." She looked up at him. "The timing is right. Could it be that simple?"

"Possibly. It's sort of a common theme. Full moon, sacrifice. It's as bad a guess as any other, I suppose."

She threw her head back in frustration. "All right. Let's go with that. Let's assume Ponlok is not already dead. Let's assume the ritual is going to happen on the night if the 7th. We don't know where, except that it will likely be somewhere in Pittsley or Sipponet. And we don't know who. We're not likely to discover where. We have to concentrate on the 'who.' They're here, somewhere in Pittsley County."

"If they live around here, we may know them. I may know them."

"But that doesn't help, does it? Unless you have some reason to think you know them."

"No," he conceded. "I have no suspicions at all."

"No," she agreed. "I don't suppose they'd be parishioners."

They sat in silence for a moment until Martin finally said, "Or would they?"

Julia looked at him quizzically.

"I think I need to talk with my predecessor." His predecessor, Reverend Benjamin Chauncy, had been minister to the Sipponet church for over twenty years before his reassignment to Groton, Connecticut. "He might know something I don't about any anti-apostolic townspeople."

Martin reached over to the phone, put it on speaker, and dialed the home of the Groton pastorate. He let the phone ring fifteen times but there was no answer. There should have been. There would only be one reason that Benjamin wouldn't answer at this hour, which Julia knew as well as Martin. Reverend Chauncy had probably passed out.

On the way home, she realized that neither she nor Cat had eaten since breakfast and she was too tired to even think about cooking. She veered off onto The Cranberry Highway, up to Route 44 to the nearest McDonald's. At the drive-thru she ordered a diet cola and the special—one quarter-pounder free with one at the regular price—and then parked on the side of the restaurant. She ate one hamburger and gave the other one, piece by piece, to Cat. She called Adam from her cell to tell him she was going home to bed.

"Just as well," he replied, "Cutter and Billy are still here. I'll see you tomorrow. By the way, how did you make out with the water heater?"

"I haven't checked yet, but Mr. Rezendes came at five o'clock on the dot. I had to leave but I'm sure he's taken care of it."

"So I'll see you tomorrow?"

"Absolutely."

She finished her soda on the way home, let Cat out into the yard, and went into the kitchen. Mr. Rezendes' bill was on the table. She stared at it, uncomprehending. He had written "250.00." That would have been just the wholesale cost of the heater. And he hadn't even charged for his labor.

She took a luxurious hot shower, letting the steam build up in the bathroom, and feeling the soothing water cascade over her face, shoulders, breasts, hips, legs, as though drawing out all of the day's tensions, so grateful to Mr. Rezendes for his kindness. Afterwards, she went directly to bed expecting to sleep as soon as she closed her eyes.

The phone rang as soon as she had settled under the covers. She debated answering but curiosity won out.

"Hi, Mom," came the girlish voice on the other end. "Just calling to see how you are."

"I'm fine, sweetheart. Everything okay there?"

"Perfect. I just wanted to let you know that Paul and I have already started on our book."

Karen went on to tell her about the story and Paul's cover illustration, and that she was going to mail Julia a copy of it so she could see it, too. Her daughter's excitement was an antidote to the day's grim events and Julia listened happily to Karen's description of what they were going to do in the weeks to come.

"We should have the first draft by the time you visit us at Christmas," Karen concluded. "You are coming, aren't you?"

"Yes," Julia answered before she allowed any doubts to seep in. "And Adam is coming with me."

"That's wonderful. I'm so glad."

The rest of the conversation was about Jesse, and after they had hung up Julia lay back and motioned Cat to come up on the bed with her.

"Maybe you can come too," she said to the dog. "So what if I have to max out my credit card? *Carpe dog*, right?"

Cat circled three times around and flopped next to her with head on the other pillow.

* * *

He was surprised to be still alive. And even more surprised that the two people in black ski masks—one who kept a pistol pointed at him—had brought him a bedroll for the floor, a pisspot, and a meal. They'd brought a plastic gallon jug of water and two submarine sandwiches of sandwich meat he had never tasted, although it was very good. He had asked them what they wanted and where he was, but neither of them spoke to him.

When they'd opened the door, he'd gotten a glimpse of light beyond and realized that he was in someone's basement. He quickly looked around the room and saw it was entirely empty except for what they had brought him. After they left, he began running his fingers over the door and explored all the walls as high as he could reach. The walls were concrete. There were no windows. The door, of course, was locked.

The only sounds he could hear were the creakings of footsteps above him and muffled voices. He couldn't make out the words, but it sounded like there were more than two people up there. Then there was silence. Then another voice and more footsteps.

He ate one sandwich and decided to save the second one for later. He didn't know how long he would be there or whether they would feed him again.

He imagined his mother praying for him in her crowded apartment of women. She had used her American wages to buy a small perfumed candle that she found in the drugstore. It was olive green, scented with sage. Along with the candle, she lit a cinnamon incense stick. It wasn't exactly right, but the fragrance reminded her of home.

She would remove her shoes, he imagined, then she would kneel in front of the statue and press her hands together at her chest and at her head. She would prostrate herself to the floor three times. Then she would chant the Namo tassa under her breath in Pali, the language of Theravada Buddhism, in homage to the Buddha.

His mother would try to prepare herself for the possibility of his death. There were no monks to lecture her on the relentless effort that is required to gain enlightenment and the difficulty of the way. But she knew the Dukkha, that suffering is universal and that the cause of suffering is human desire and the obstinate clinging to transience, to things that are of the world and not of the spirit. Only by achieving Nirvana would suffering cease. And only through the Eightfold Path would one achieve Nirvana.

"The world is merely samsara," he repeated—a cycle of birth and death. He started to count The Eightfold Path on his fingers: right knowledge; right attitude; right speech; right action; right livelihood; right effort; right mindfulness; right meditation. He chanted under his breath.

Wednesday, October 4th

A few minutes before eight a.m., Julia went back to Martin's office on her way to work. She was too impatient to wait to hear his conversation with Benjamin Chauncy second-hand. Whether or not he had been drinking the night before, Benjamin would be on duty the next morning; of this Martin said, he was certain. Whatever was driving his predecessor, he would not neglect his parish duties.

They sat watching the clock. When it read 8:05 a.m., Martin dialed the Groton number again, and again put the phone on speaker.

On the fourth ring, a man's voice answered. "South Congregational Church. Reverend Chauncy speaking."

Julia and Martin exchanged satisfied looks.

"Benjamin? Martin Ryman."

"Martin," repeated the older man, warmly. "It's good to hear from you. How are you?"

"I'm well, Benjamin, and you?"

"Busy, as usual. You know how it is. Church suppers, church breakfasts, marriages, christenings, sick calls, and funerals. It never ends. How are things in Sipponet?"

"Actually, that's what I'm calling about. Well, not exclusively Sipponet. There's been another disappearance of another young child in the area. In Pittsley."

"Oh?"

"Yes," Martin continued. "A young Cambodian boy, Ponlok Nim, working on Amos Hall's bog."

"A boy, you say?"

Julia thought she detected a sense of relief in the reply. Or was she reading too much into it?

"I'm very sorry to hear that," continued Rev. Chauncy. "When you say 'disappearance,' do you mean lost?"

"It's uncertain." Martin raised his eyebrows at Julia and plunged in. "I was hoping you might have some information that could help us."

"Me?"

"Yes. There's a possibility that this might be a kidnapping. A cult abduction, like before."

There was a pause on the other end and Julia gestured for Martin to continue but Chauncy responded, "I understood that the previous abductions were of young girls."

"That's true. But we think this may have been a mistake. From a distance, the young boy could possibly have been mistaken for a girl."

There was silence again on the other end of the line before Chauncy said, "Does that seem likely?"

"I don't know," Martin said. "But that's all we have to go on right now. And if it is the same group of men, they're probably here in the area. That's why I'm calling you, Benjamin. You lived here most of your life. You know most of these people better than I do."

Chauncy coughed then replied, "I really haven't kept in contact with anyone."

Martin leaned closer to the phone. "But some of the earlier abductions took place while you were still here. So I thought you might have heard something back then."

"Not that I can think of," Chauncy responded directly. "I never heard anything about it. I still wouldn't even know about Nicole Fayette, except for that woman you sent to see me."

"You mean Julia Arnault." Martin glanced at her.

"That's it, Dr. Arnault. But of course Nicole's murder took place a very long time ago."

"So you heard that they caught the murderer, Marvel Kane?"

"Yes, I read that."

Was there a note of reservation in Benjamin's voice? Julia thought.

Marvel Kane had been the mayor of Sipponet, as was his father before him, Mayor Usha Kane. It had made headlines all over the region when Marvel was convicted of killing his then-girlfriend some two decades earlier. His wife—who hadn't known of the affair at the time—had since divorced him. Less because of the illicit liaison, people speculated, than because he had fathered a child who was a living reminder of the scandal. His wife had since moved away from Sipponet and only her own children knew of her current whereabouts.

Julia quickly scribbled 'Sherry' on his note pad and pointed to it.

Martin nodded and said into the speaker, "Did you know that Marvel had a child on the side? Cheryl?"

"Not at the time."

"But you knew about Nicole and Marvel?"

"No. Of course not."

Julia gestured for him to move one. This was a dead end.

Martin paused. "If there is a cult in Pittsley county, Benjamin, would you have any idea who might be involved?"

"No idea whatsoever."

"Anyone that might go down that path?"

"None that I know of."

Did he answer too quickly? Julia wondered.

"Well...would you give it some thought?"

"I will give it some thought. But if there is a cult, I'm sure I can't think of anyone I know who would belong to it."

"I suppose we could be barking up the wrong tree." Martin shrugged at Julia.

"Perhaps so. I'm sorry I can't help you. What was the boy's name, Bonluck?"

"Ponlok. His friends call him Lucky."

"Lucky," the reverend repeated without inflection. "Maybe he'll turn up."

"I hope to God he will."

"Yes. We'll pray on it."

"Well, take care of yourself, Benjamin."

"You, too, Martin. Keep in touch."

"I will." Martin hung up, disquieted, and turned to Julia. "Did that sound kosher to you? So to speak."

Julia shook her head. "I don't know him as well as you do, but something seemed off." It was a sense of his pauses and replies that gave her the same apprehensive feeling she'd had about the man in the airport.

"To me, too." Martin concurred.

"Perhaps he would be more candid in person," she suggested.

"I think that's a good idea. The problem is," he consulted his calendar, "I have a baptism this morning, a wedding later today, and a funeral tomorrow morning. I wouldn't be able to get there until tomorrow afternoon...no...I've got a confirmation class tomorrow afternoon."

"I could go," Julia offered. "Not today, but I can arrange my schedule tomorrow to be able to go there in the morning. He knows me. Maybe I can get something out of him. If not, then you can follow-up. What do you think?"

Martin shrugged. "That's how it will have to be."

Julia left Martin's office right after the call intending to go straight to work. But on her way to work, she had an impulse to visit Tessa's grave. It wasn't very far and there was enough time to still get to her first appointment.

She parked at the gate and walked up the path to the grave.

"Hi, Tessa, its Julia." That was kind of silly, thought. She took a lingering breath of the cool air and looked around. The leaves on the trees were bright with sun-dappled colors. In a few days they would peak and then it would be all over.

"I'm sorry you'll miss your trip to Vermont this year."

Tessa always looked forward to the family's annual foliage pilgrimage. On their drive north, she and B.J. would describe everything they saw along the way so that Billy could visualize it, too. Then they would stop at the Barstow Farm for Macoun apples and fresh cider, and bring home arm-sized pumpkins for pie-making and jugs of maple syrup for pancakes. Each year, she would find a new place for their picnic lunch, always near water. And on the way home, they would play their favorite music CDs and sing along together. Autumn was Tessa's favorite time of year.

But the truth was, autumn just meant the leaves were in a death throe. Even this early, they were beginning drift down onto the ground like burnt paper. Tessa used to pick up the ones with the most color, the reddest maple leaves, and iron them between sheets of waxed paper and make little note cards with the leaves as decoration.

"I still have your notecards, Tessa."

She used to love cranberries, too, Julia thought. Tessa made cranberry-nut bread, and cranberry-orange relish, apple-cranberry pie, brandied cranberries, and every chicken dish had cranberries in it somewhere.

"I know red is your favorite color."

Julia had bought Tessa's funeral dress. Billy told her to pick out something his wife would like so she selected the reddest dress she could find. Tessa looked beautiful in it. Julia wished Tessa could have had had such a dress while she was alive. Her eyes began to moisten and she wiped them dry and looked away from the headstone on which was inscribed Tessa's name and dates, "Beloved Wife and Mother," and a treble clef with a series of notes under which was inscribed, "Never a Wrong Note."

Julia's gaze strayed over the rows of graves, to the stone wall that separated the Pittsley Cemetery from Leroy Bingham's back field. She wondered what that black van was doing at the rear of the cemetery. She saw a break in the wall that she hadn't noticed before. Perhaps they were repairing it.

She could see two men but not clearly, one short and the other tall. They were wearing grey hooded sweatshirts. But they weren't repairing the wall. They were loading what was obviously a young goat into the back of the van. They had tied its muzzle and were pulling it up a ramp. Then they closed the van doors and piled up the rocks back in position to complete the wall. After that, they got back into the van and drove the rear cemetery road around the perimeter and out onto the street.

Julia could hardly believe what she had just seen. Were the men stealing the goat? Or were they loading it into the van to take it somewhere with Mr. Bingham's permission? But shouldn't Leroy Bingham have been there then?

Maybe she should try to get a license plate number. She hurried back to her car and drove swiftly down the open grassy rows of graves, apologizing to the residents under her breath as she went. She reached the gate just as the van pulled out onto the street. She was pretty sure they hadn't seen her. She could only read a portion of the Massachusetts license plate. Maybe it would be enough. It was so unsettling she decided to call Adam as soon as she got into her office.

* * *

Within twenty minutes of Julia's call, Adam sat across from Chief Burke in the cramped run-down station office. "Can you run the license plate for me? It's only a partial but with Julia's description of the van, it should be easy enough to make."

When Carson Burke first arrived in Pittsley about three years ago, he'd come out of the Dover Heights suburban police station. The crime there had been routine, mostly breaking and entering in the affluent homes with their wall safes, pools, au pairs, and gardeners. He'd told the interviewing committee that he'd grown tired of the bankers and corporate CEOs (and that was just the wives) and all the snob politics. Here in Pittsley, he would have expected the traffic violations, drug-induced thievery, marital disputes, and weekly brawls. What he obviously did not expect, Adam thought, was the child murders he'd encountered his first month on the job. And now there was the disappearance of yet another child. And what he definitely did not expect, or want, was another complaint by Adam Sabeski that somebody's goat had been stolen.

Adam glanced toward the open window overlooking the parking lot. The temperature had risen to the high sixties. Perfect. In summer, the air conditioning never worked right. In winter, the heat was either too high or too low. There was only one holding cell in the station, the evidence room was as insecure as a public toilet, and the entire building could fit into one level of the new look-at-me houses around town.

"Adam, it's a *goat*."

"I talked to Leroy Bingham. It's more than one goat. It's his third. And a calf from the Galloway Farm and one from Delany's."

"Yeah, all right. I'll have Percy run it."

"I thought he retired a couple of months ago."

"I've been assigning him details. He still comes in every day."

"Here?"

Burke shrugged. "He practically opens up the office. Comes in, makes coffee for the men. Hangs around for a couple of hours. I think his wife is glad to have him out of her hair."

Adam smiled sympathetically. "Well, he's an old warhorse. He probably doesn't know what to do with himself."

"I think he's still looking around the woods for signs of the Cambodian boy on his own time."

"Any clues?"

Burke shook his head. "It's in the hands of the Staties now."

He knew Burke had no love for the State Police; but he had to concede they had more equipment, more officers, and better technology.

"Disenchanted, are we?" Adam said.

"You know how it is, they treat us like yokels. Most of our unit are good, reliable officers. We may've had a few bad apples—"

Burke left the rest unsaid. His predecessor, Bill Kerwin, had been a good old boy who was respected by almost everyone, but he'd been "remiss," they put it kindly, in following-up on the missing children over the years. And he hadn't exactly been minding the store, "not to speak ill of the dead," when he should have. Everyone knew there'd been some scandals in the past with some of the old guard skimming a bit here and there, and even an indictment. But Burke was trying to get beyond that with new hires and better training. He was doing a decent job of it by all accounts, but maybe if they had a modern police station, things would be different.

"You're not closing the book on Ponlok, are you?"

"Hell, no." Burke answered.

"Good," Adam said. "And about the other thing, have Perce call me when he gets something, okay?"

"Will do." As Adam got up to leave, Burke added, "So what's going on down at the Legion tonight? Do I need to put somebody there on detail?"

"No. Just a meeting. You know about that eminent domain thing?"

Burke nodded.

"You hear anything about what the town is planning?"

"Nope," Burke put his hands behind his head. "I'm only a mushroom. They keep me in the dark and feed me shit. But let me know, will you?"

"I will."

By six fifty-five p.m., the small Legion hall was full. Adam stood to the side of the podium with Max Kipper. Pictures of all the past Commanders looked down at them from the pine-paneled wall. Adam wondered what they'd think of tonight's gathering. He believed they'd approve.

Chairs had been added in rows, theatre style, to accommodate the nearly eighty people. From their viewpoint on the podium, the larger group of Juckets sat on the left side of the room facing the stage, bog men and Fiona on the other side. Each group talked only among themselves in low voices.

"You're sure about this, Kip?" Adam asked as they stood to the side.

Kip gave him a withering look.

"I know you're sure, but it's—" Adam shook his head, "—hard to believe."

"Believe it."

"But isn't that illegal?"

"Nope. They're quite legal bandits."

Kip looked at his watch and mounted the dais. He quieted the crowd by tapping his finger on the microphone. It had an immediate effect.

"Good evening," he said perfunctorily. "I'm attorney Maxwell Kipper. As most of you know, I was born and raised here in Pittsley. I've been engaged by Amos Hall to represent him regarding a letter that he recently received from the Town announcing the potential taking of his land by eminent domain."

Kip acknowledged his client, seated on the first aisle seat. Then he looked towards the Juckets. "I understand that many of you also received such a letter."

"All of us!" Elgin Bradburn, in the first seat in the first row on the Jucket side, across from Amos, stood up. One by one, hands alongside him and behind were raised.

Arlo Tulliver sat in the last row, but did not raise his hand. Cutter and Billy sat next to him.

"I understand that Adam Sabeski and Elmer Goodson and his friends, Cutter Briggs and Billy Jensen, have met with you," Kip focused again on the Juckets, "and explained the situation as it exists."

Amid nods from everyone, Kip continued, "With Amos' consent, I'm here tonight to share with you what I've learned about this matter." He paused before delivering the blow. "To reiterate, according to the plans I have seen, all of your homes," he looked toward the Juckets, "as well as Amos Hall's bog are under order to be seized by eminent domain, and you are to be given fair market value in exchange. This has been approved by the Commonwealth"

Amidst the reactions of "NO WAY!" and "Who the hell do they think they are?" Amos Hall stood up.

"Quiet down, everybody, Amos has a question."

Gradually, the angry voices subsided. Kip nodded to his client.

"*Why* us?"

Kip raised his voice quieting the murmuring. "Amos asked an important question. Why *your* land? From what I have learned, it is clear to me there are four reasons why they've selected your land as opposed to any other. The first three reasons are location, location, location. Your land borders Lake Tipisquin, which makes it desirable in itself. But it's also accessible to The Cranberry Highway, which makes it prime property for business development." He paused for a beat. "The fourth reason is political. They don't think you have enough clout to oppose it." He waited another second before adding, "And—you—don't."

More comments flew among the Juckets about clout and what they would do with it.

"But," Kip said loudly and waited until they turned their attention back to him, "there's another question you should be asking." They became silent. "We discussed the 'why,' but we haven't talked about the 'what.' What is the reason? What do they intend to do with this land?" He paused again for effect. "Based on the plans I've seen and my conversations with various government officials," he did not feel it necessary to include contacts at the State House by name, "I am given to understand that the Town of Pittsley has agreed to allow a private development corporation to build a golf course and hotel around Lake Tipisquin—"

"The HELL they will!"

"How can they do that?"

"—*and*," Kip continued stridently, "that this is a core area of what will be a larger resort and casino, intended to become a regional tourist attraction."

The hall erupted with Anglo-Saxon plosives ending in c-k.

"If anybody so much as puts a foot on my land," Elgin shouted, "I'll blow their damned heads off." The rest of the Juckets cheered.

Kip waited.

Adam was keenly aware that the other side of the room had remained deadly quiet. Although himself a Jucket—and entirely respectful of their boisterous anger—if he were to pick the group not to be trifled with, it would have been the bog men. Their anger was fierce and threatening whereas the Juckets wanted immediate action.

His mind darted to the story Kip said he used to tell at Harvard alumni dinners to his law colleagues. It was a way of defining himself. 'A guy I know,' he'd say, 'was driving on a country road one night in his old pickup. Suddenly, he smashed into a wild turkey. He lost control, drove off the road and hit a tree head-on. What's the first question you'd ask? Well, I'll tell you. Any normal person would ask, "Was he injured?" Right? But you guys,' meaning the lawyers at his table, would ask, "Does he have insurance, and how much did he hurt the tree?"' At which point, his listeners would laugh politely. However, Kip wasn't finished. 'Now where I come from, we see things a little differently. A Swamp Yankee, the first thing he'll ask is, "What's he want for the truck?"' More polite laughter as he continued. 'A bog man won't ask anything. He'll just watch and assess and figure the guy was drunk, which he was. But a Jucket, the first thing a Jucket will ask is *"Did he get the turkey?"* The laughter was genuine now and Kip would conclude, '"And yes I did, and it tasted fine."' He said they never quite knew how to react to that.

As the noise dwindled, Fiona Hathaway stood up.

"I have another question. 'Who?' Who is the developer behind this?"

"Good question," Kip said. "The answer to that took a little research. On paper, it's the Parkwood Development Corporation."

"On paper?" she repeated.

Gradually eyes turned towards Cutter, who flinched.

"Oh no," Cutter responded. "It may be a casino but it's not Indians, that much I know. If it were, I'd get a slice of that money pie."

"Correct," Kip said, gathering back the audience's attention. "Parkwood is a corporation within a corporation within a corporation. We had to trace back four levels to find the actual principals of the company."

"And they are?" Fiona persisted.

Kip pulled a folded paper from his pocket, unfolded it, and placed it on the dais. All eyes were riveted on him. He read the names on the paper as though they were courtroom indictments.

"Conny Cranshaw, president. Dennis Buckley, vice-president. Robert Carriou, treasurer."

Pandemonium broke out again.

Conny Cranshaw was a trucking company owner and hometown developer who had already ravaged most of the town's available land along with builder Dennis Buckley; Robert Carriou was the ne'er-do-well brother of Albert Carriou, Pittsley Selectman. Not carpetbaggers, but all native sons in Pittsley County and all known to the audience.

"Those sons-of-bitches!"

"Conny-sucking-Cranshaw, we should have known it!"

Kip pressed his hands out in front of him, palms up, like a traffic cop slowing speeders.

When the noise subdued, Fiona sat down, saying, "That nest of vipers," she said. "Now what do we do?"

Kip cleared his throat. "I can only advise you on the legal process. If you would like to make this a class-action suit, I'm willing to represent you. You can contact me individually or appoint a spokesman for the group. I must tell you, however, that legally, it's not winnable. There is very little I can do in court unless the State initiates legislative action to remedy the problem. I also feel there is not much likelihood of that happening."

The room fell into a desperate silence.

"While the extent of my involvement must be limited to trying to persuade the courts and the lawmakers that this land-seizure is an unjust hardship on property owners, I believe Adam Sabeski has something to add in my absence."

Kip stepped down and walked up the aisle between the two groups and out the door. All heads turned to follow him as he left the hall, then turned back expectantly to Adam as he mounted the podium.

"We all know well enough that the legal process takes time," Adam began when Kip was out of earshot.

"There ain't no time," Elgin interrupted.

"I know that. So we're going to have to help it along a little."

"How?" asked Fiona.

"As Thomas Jefferson said," he began, "'A little rebellion now and then is a good thing. It is a medicine necessary for the sound health of government.' We still have the spirit of rebellion in us, don't we? It's in our history. In our souls. In our soil. It's not just the history of the American Revolution, but also the history of Massachusetts. We have never laid down to oppression."

Adam looked around at the paintings on the wall. There were no native Americans, no African-Americans, no minorities of any stripe. But he realized that this was not the time to discourse on the wrongs of colonial or American society. His purpose was to move this audience to coordinated action. He mentally apologized to his former American Civilization professor and launched into the shorthand version of history.

"For those of you who aren't familiar with Shays' Rebellion, that uprising also took place in western Massachusetts in 1786-87. Ten years after independence, the economy of the country was chaotic. The 'paper money' had no stable backing. Property taxes were excessive. Farmers were faced with selling off their land below market value and if they did, they could lose the right to vote. Those who didn't sell and couldn't pay their debts were thrown into prison by the courts. These were many of the same men who fought in the American Revolution. Daniel Shays, himself a veteran of the Revolution, marshaled not only the farmers but also the sympathetic townspeople. They shut down the courts and protested the unfair imprisonment of the farmers. Peacefully, at first, then with weapons."

"I believe they lost," Amos Hall interjected dryly.

"Yes" Adam answered, "they lost the battle. But they won the cause. When Shays' rag-tag army of 600 attempted to attack the Springfield arsenal, they were outnumbered by 4,400 Springfield and Boston militia. It was a rout but it made the federal government sit up and take notice. It soon moved to drop the Articles of Confederation and adopt the United States Constitution and to issue a single currency backed with gold. And although there were some casualties in the rebellion, Shays was ultimately pardoned by the new governor, John Hancock. So, because of their uprising, our entire system of government changed."

"That was over two hundred years ago," Amos said.

"I don't think we're inclined to take up arms against the government," Isaac Lovell added.

After a short silence, Fiona stood up again and waved her hand over the crowd. "What's the matter with you boys? I'll tell you right now, if you haven't got the berries to fight this, *I* have." She thrust her forefinger up in the air. "And if it takes a gun, then a gun it is!"

"Calm down, Fiona," Adam said. "I'm not suggesting we do it that way. But we have to make some sort of rebellion. We came up with an idea of how we can get some attention on this—that is, Cutter did—and maybe delay it long enough to let Kip do his work. It doesn't involve risking your life, but it might bend a by-law or two." Adam looked around the room. "If you've got the spirit for it."

In the quiet that followed, slowly Elgin Bradburn rose to his feet opposite Fiona. Nothing was said, but one by one all the Juckets rose to stand with him.

Amos was the first to stand up on the opposite side of the room next to Fiona, followed by each of the bog men.

"Up in back," Adam inclined his head toward the last row of Juckets, "Cutter Briggs and Billy Jensen are going to help organize this. Cutter, you stay on that side. Billy, you come over here. We're going to make some suggestions, you're going to make some suggestions, and together we're going to work up a plan of action. I'll move around the room and make sure we're all on the same page. You know and I know that if they can do this to any of us, they can do it to all of us. The bottom line is—we will NOT let this happen in Pittsley."

"Damn right, we won't," said Elgin, looking toward Fiona. She, in turn, gave an affirmative nod back.

* * *

It was almost eleven o'clock by the time Adam arrived at Julia's house, saying, "I probably should have gone home and crashed. I'm really tired. But I promised I'd come by after the meeting. And I missed not seeing you yesterday."

They sat out on the deck she'd had screened in last Spring in anticipation of the Summer flies and mosquitoes. She had just put up the storm windows earlier that evening and plugged in the electric heater to take the chill off—the temperature was falling fast. With Cat curled up on the lounge, she and Adam sat side-by-side in cushioned wicker armchairs she had painted a forest green.

She reached over and rubbed his shoulders. His muscles were tight. In the woods beyond her lawn, a barn owl hooted. The cicadas kept up their boisterous din. Small bats flew back and forth catching insects in the bright moonlight. In the near distance, several overlaying howls announced the coyotes.

Cat picked up her head and listened, her nose moving to catch the scent. Then, deciding there was no threat, she lay her head down again on her paws.

"They're back," Adam commented, meaning the coyotes. "I'd love to put a tracking collar on one some day to see where they go. They can range thirty miles or more."

They sat quietly for a while listening to the night sounds until Julia asked, "Are you hungry?"

"No, but I'll have some coffee if you've already made it."

She not only had coffee ready, she'd made a pumpkin cheesecake with maple-soaked pecans. Her disappointment at his refusal must have registered on her face because he wound up with a huge slice of the cheesecake.

"Aren't you going to have any?" he asked.

She couldn't wait to taste it but prudence ruled and she took only a small slice. It was getting so hard to keep her appetite in check. Was it just one more delightful side effect of menopause? However, she realized, she only got this hungry around Adam. Hmmm.

"So how did the meeting go?" she asked, denying to herself that she had any real anxiety about their relationship.

"Everybody showed up. I think it went well. We're keeping it close to the vest until we get it all worked out."

"So you're not going to tell me?"

"I will. As soon as we have everything in place. We all made a promise not to say anything to anybody until then."

"What did Kip find out about this Parkwood Corporation, can you tell me that much?"

"The principals are local. Including Conny Cranshaw."

Julia made a face. It seemed like Conny Cranshaw was behind everything that conspired to rob Pittsley of its small town character. He'd bought up most of the vacant land, put in developments that stretched the town's budget, affected the water resources, and crowded the schools. She knew of two instances personally where he'd conned elderly people out of their property—one of them, the widow down the road from her. Conny was well named.

"He wants to put in a resort and casino," Adam continued.

She almost tipped her plate over. "A casino? Here? And the town's going to let him?"

"Not let him," Adam said tonelessly, "encourage him."

Julia shook her head and stared at the sky. The moon was so large. Nearly full. Her thoughts drifted to Ponlok Nim. Where was he tonight? Was he even alive?

Her thoughts were interrupted by Adam saying, "Change of subject. What's going on with your offer to partner with Alonzo? Have you talked to him today?"

"No."

Adam looked at her quizzically.

"Maybe I should be doing something else."

"Like what?"

Adam put his feet on the coffeetable and she almost asked him to take them off, then mentally admonished herself. After all, it was a deck table, not a good piece of furniture. Did she really care that he had his feet on the table? No. She really didn't.

"Let's talk about it tomorrow," she replied. "Right now I'd rather go to bed."

"Fine with me. But I warn you, I may be a little too tired to meet your expectations tonight."

"Wanna bet?" she said, with a low, provocative laugh.

* * *

Upstairs from their captive, Usha Kane paced in silence. Eight other men sat in a circle in his livingroom. Had Lucky been able to see them, he would not have known even one of them, not even Usha Kane, the former mayor of Sipponet. He would not have known that these men were from Pittsley and the surrounding towns. Or that there originally had been thirteen members of the group, including Usha's son, Marvel—now imprisoned with another of their group, Joe Woods, for the murder of Nicole Fayette. Or that that particular murder had begun this preternatural alliance twenty-one years ago. Or that this alliance had been responsible for the murder or eight young girls since then, the last one being Jeannine Bradburn.

"I have wrestled with this for the past two days," Usha was saying. *"I have prayed to God to ask for guidance. And He has answered me."*

The other men looked at him expectantly.

"Genesis 22: 9," Usha announced. *'And they came to the place which God had told him of; and Abraham built an altar there, and laid the wood in order, and bound Isaac his son, and laid him on the altar upon the wood.'"*

"What does that tell us?" he asked.

"Abraham was going to sacrifice his son," Dennis Buckley shrugged. *"But God stopped him."*

"What it tells us," Usha said impatiently, *"is that God accepts the sacrifice of boys."*

Thursday, October 5th

Julia was still asleep when Adam awoke around six a.m. He slipped out of bed, showered, and dressed without waking her.

Downstairs, he put on a fresh pot of coffee and Cat meandered into the kitchen and went to the back door. The dog looked at him meaningfully and he chuckled as he let her out. She does make her needs known, he thought amiably, just like her mistress. Meanwhile he fixed Cat's breakfast—a mixture of weight-control kibble, some boiled chicken he found in a plastic container, a dash of olive oil, a splash of warm water, and a small pinch of garlic powder. By the time he was finished, Cat had come back in the open door and sat down to wait. He put her stainless steel bowl with "Cat" engraved on it in front of her and the dog gulped down the contents.

Now, what should he make for their breakfast? He saw a half-dozen of fresh eggs from the Galloway Farm in the fridge. That was a start. What else? All Julia's salad makings—fresh baby spinach, tomatoes, Bermuda onions, and mushrooms. There was some Jarlsberg in the cheese drawer. He could make a frittata. And did she have any tubes of biscuit dough? Yes. Perfect.

As he put the frittata and buttermilk biscuits in the oven, he heard the shower going. He quickly set the table.

Adam's timing was just right or rather, he thought, Julia's timing was just right. She came down just as he was pulling breakfast out of the oven.

"Good morning," he said brightly.

"Good morning. You made breakfast? Smells terrific." She looked at the array of food on the table. "Thank you for this. I'll do the cleaning up in trade."

"Deal." He sat down to eat with her. "I put last night's dishes in the dishwasher."

"I knew you were a keeper," she said as she tasted the frittata. "This is good."

He was more pleased than he let on. "So tell me," he said between bites, "about your qualms about going with Alonzo. We sort of left it in the middle last night." He grinned suggestively and she flashed him a quick smile.

Between mouthfuls, she answered, "It was something Sam said. About what he thinks I really like doing."

"Which is?"

"Working with victims. Doing investigating. Psychological investigation. Forensic psychology, I guess."

Adam took a deep breath and said nothing.

"What? You disagree?" she said.

He realized that wasn't the reaction she'd expected. "No. It's not that. It's just that working in the criminal justice system can be pretty frustrating. What exactly did you have in mind?"

"I'm not sure. Community practice doesn't excite me."

Adam turned his attention to his food, not wanting to say the wrong thing. "You have a good position at the hospital. You might not want to give up all those benefits."

"Well...aren't we practical?"

Her voice was icy, so he tried to recover. "I guess it's just my protective side."

After a pause she answered, "You're right, I suppose. I do have to have a steady income. I can't afford to take chances with that. After all, I don't suppose we're ever going to get married, are we? This is delicious, by the way."

Adam froze. "I...er...," he faltered. "I didn't know that was on the table. Marriage." The words hung in the air like wet clothes on a line. "Is that what you want?"

She looked at him steadily. "I think what I want is to believe we'll always be there for each other." Then she added lightly, "Even when we're old and sexually inactive."

He decided to duck the marriage question. "You think I'll be sexually inactive some day?"

"I said 'we.'"

"What makes you think we—"

"Off topic," she interrupted. "Never mind. Sorry. Back to the issue. The fact is, I don't see us living together in the same house."

He took an inadvertent breath of relief.

"Neither do you, I gather," she said. "Maybe when we get older—"

"There's that word again," he said.

"Then, maybe," she continued, "maybe we will want to share a home. But I don't see it happening right now, do you?"

"I hadn't thought about it." Oh, man, he thought, how do I get past this?

"Sure you have. That's why you practically hyperventilated when I began this subject. Anyway, I was thinking we could be engaged. That would cover it, wouldn't it?"

"I guess so," he said numbly. He felt his appetite dwindling.

"I don't need a ring or anything. We can just decide we're engaged."

"If that would satisfy you." He put down his fork.

"Yes. It would." She got up and poured them each a cup of coffee. As she put the cups on the table, she said, "By the way, I saw Martin on Tuesday. About Ponlok."

"Oh?"

He knew his voice sounded wary and he couldn't help it. He was still sensitive about the fact that she dated Martin during her short break-up with him. He had never asked her any details and she never provided any other than it had been quite casual, just a dinner here and there, although Martin would have liked it to develop into something more.

"First," she continued as she added milk to her coffee, "I went to see Chaya Nim. The missing boy's mother."

"And?" Adam said in relief that she had moved on. He took a big gulp of his black coffee.

"I wanted to look at a photo of her son after Sam suggested that perhaps Ponlok's abduction was a mistake."

"We don't know that he was abducted," he corrected her.

"We didn't know that Jeannine Bradburn was abducted either, until I found her body," she said, unblinking.

Chastened, he nodded. "All right. What kind of mistake?"

"Sam suggested it. And when I saw Ponlok's picture, it convinced me that they might have thought he was a girl—at least at first. Mrs. Nim had cut his hair but it was still long. I think she didn't want him to become just another American teenager so fast. And when I asked what he was wearing when he was working in the bog, and she said he had on pants and a top just like hers."

"And where does Martin come into this?" He said this more snappishly than he intended but Julia charged on.

"I believe that we're dealing with the same group of men who took Jeannine and the other girls. So I went to Martin to ask him more about cult behavior."

"Such as?"

"Such as who they could be and what they might be planning to do with Ponlok."

"And?"

She went on to explain that if it was a cult abduction, they knew at least two of the members were local: Floyd Mather and Babe Hampley. It was too bad they're dead and never told them anything—but if two of them were from Pittsley, it's likely the rest are from this area, too. She told him that Martin had called Benjamin Chauncy to see if he had any idea who the others might be. Chauncy grew up in Pittsley and was in the Sipponet parish for a very long time.

"He knows just about everybody, including the Fayette family," she said. "He knew Nicole Fayette's murderers. Maybe it's all tied together. Reverend Chauncy said he doesn't know anything, but Martin's not convinced. So I'm just going into my office for an hour this morning, then I'm driving down to Connecticut to speak with him because Martin can't get away."

"That's all pretty far-fetched, isn't it, Julia?" He finished his coffee and put the empty cup into the sink.

"But it feels right. I can't tell you why. We were trying to figure out what would be the likely date for a ceremony, assuming it would be earlier in the month rather than later. What we came up with is the full moon this Saturday. The day after tomorrow."

Adam had begun to tune her out, preoccupied now with this morning's meeting with Amos Hall. They would have to move fast or this thing could be over before they had a chance to stop it. They'd have to do a lot of organizing and coordinating for it to work.

"What are you thinking," she interrupted. "You seem a million miles away."

"Sorry, Julia, but I've got to leave. I've got a lot to do today." Did that sound like a brush-off? He didn't mean it to. "Let's talk more tonight."

She squinted at him. "Were you even listening to me?"

"Yes. You're going to see Benjamin Chauncy. You can fill me in tonight, okay?"

"Okay," she said perfunctorily.

"Don't be mad at me. I wouldn't leave if I didn't have to."

"I know," she said, her voice softening. "Thank you for breakfast, it was sweet of you to do that."

"Oh, yes," he said as he bent over her, "I gave Cat her breakfast, too."

"Good man." She lifted her face towards him.

He gave her a swift kiss on the lips. He'd make it all up to her later.

By the time he reached Amos' house, there were trucks and cars lining the driveway and on the road in front.

Inside, Adam joined and the contingent of bog men in his livingroom. The original group of seven had grown to nearly twenty, everyone who had been at the meeting last night.

"There are at least a hundred more who will help out," Fiona announced. "Everyone in the Association is behind you, Amos."

"I phoned my cousin in New Jersey," Isaac Lovell said. "He's going to send out the call. They'll be coming up."

"I need to know exactly who is coming and from where in order to set up a schedule," Adam said, using the pad and pen Amos had provided.

"You know," Amos remarked solemnly to the room of people, "we might go to jail for this."

"Then they'll be no cranberry sauce for Thanksgiving," Fiona answered for all of them. "We're all in this together."

"But how are we going to do this before we get stopped?" Isaac asked turning to Adam.

"We'll have everything ready by tomorrow night. Cutter and Billy are with the woodchoppers right now." He used 'woodchoppers' instead of Juckets not just because most of them were, but also because it seemed less divisive, and in this instance, more relevant. "We'll coordinate the whole thing right after this."

* * *

Julia arrived at her office early and put everything in order so that she could drive down to Connecticut for the morning. She was irritated that Adam hadn't taken her more seriously, but in truth, she knew how utterly implausible it all sounded. Grasping at straws, really. In fact, it was so unlikely, she regretted having offered to drive down to Groton on what was bound to be a wild goose chase. So much for her good instincts. But she'd promised Martin and she felt obligated to go.

There was one thing yet to do before she left. She stared at the telephone, knowing she should call Raymond Alonzo. She needed to give him an answer. Shouldn't keep him waiting. It was a once-in-a-lifetime offer. With private practice, her income would more than meet her needs. It would be foolish to turn it down. She wouldn't have to worry anymore about trips to California or new appliances if she took the job. She should take the offer. Yes.

She dialed his number and waited for his secretary to put her through.

"Hello, Julia." The voice on the other end sounded friendly yet formal.

"Hello, Alonzo. I didn't want to leave you hanging about my decision. I know you have to go forward with your plans." She nervously rubbed her fingers over the surface of her desk.

"Yes," he replied.

She sighed audibly.

"I take it that means 'no.'"

She blinked hard. Was this another mis-step she was making? "I'm sorry. I don't want you to think I don't appreciate the opportunity you've given me. But it's not what I really want right now."

"I understand."

He sounded so noncommittal. He didn't ask her why and Julia didn't really know what else to say. Why was she feeling so guilty? He would probably just go to the next person on his list.

"Thank you again for your offer, Alonzo. I want to extend my best wishes for your new practice. Perhaps we can get together for coffee some time when you've settled in."

"Indeed. Thank you for letting me know. Tell Sam I said hello."

"I will."

"Goodbye and good luck with your work, Julia."

"You, too. 'Bye now."

Hanging up, she breathed deeply. Well, she definitely burned that bridge. She hoped she'd made the right decision.

When Julia arrived at the Groton parish house, the first thing she saw was a black wreath on the door. She instantly got a feeling of foreboding in the pit of her stomach.

The housekeeper opened the door on his second knock, a short African-American woman in her seventies with cropped white hair. Her eyes were red and swollen above a small nose and mouth that almost disappeared into her chubby face.

"I'm Dr. Julia Arnault. I'm a friend of Reverend Ryman's, in Sipponet. I was hoping to see Reverend Chauncy."

"Please come in. I'm Mrs. Clarke."

Julia followed her into the hallway. The house seemed unnaturally quiet. But then, didn't all parish houses?

"Is the Reverend here? I can wait if he's out."

As Mrs. Clarke stood with Julia in the foyer, she bit her lips. "I'm sorry to tell you that Reverend Chauncy has passed."

"Passed?" Julia hesitated.

"Yes." There was a catch in Mrs. Clarke's voice.

"The Reverend's dead?"

Mrs. Clarke nodded and put her handkerchief to her eyes.

Julia rubbed her forehead. "I can't believe it. We just spoke with him yesterday. Pastor Ryman did, that is. He sounded fine."

"It was very…sudden."

"Was it a heart attack?"

"No." Her wet eyes wandered towards the study.

"An accident?"

"No." Then Mrs. Clarke shook her head and lowered her chin. "I found him early this morning. The Reverend…."

Julia finally sensed what she was trying to say. "Did Reverend Chauncy take his own life?"

Mrs. Clarke began sobbing. "It was terrible, so terrible. He hung himself. I don't know why. So terrible."

"I'm so very sorry. It must have been a great shock to you, finding him that way."

"Oh, yes," Mrs. Clarke whispered.

Julia's mind was racing. Why would Benjamin Chauncy kill himself? Did it have anything to do with the phone call? How could that be?

"You called the police?"

"They just left a little while ago. With the coroner. Then I put the wreath…." She began sobbing again.

"Perhaps you shouldn't be here alone, Mrs. Clarke."

She wiped her eyes. "I was just straightening up a little. I'm going home now."

"Did he have any next-of-kin?" She didn't know very much about him. Martin had told her he'd never married, but perhaps he had a family. "I could call them."

Mrs. Clarke shook her head. "There's no one. No family. I should call Mr. Beams. He's the head of the congregation."

"Yes. When you get home."

Julia produced her card and asked her to ask Mr. Beams to let her know of the funeral arrangements so she could tell Pastor Ryman.

"The Reverend was such a wonderful man," said Mrs. Clarke. "He was such a help to everyone. We all loved him. I don't understand. To do such a thing. I know he wrestled with his own demons—"

"You mean the drinking?" Julia said compassionately.

Mrs. Clarke looked at her in surprise. "You knew that?"

"I suspected."

She sighed deeply. "He tried to overcome it. He tried so hard. Maybe that's why—" She put her blue-laced handkerchief to her eyes again.

"Did he leave any explanation? A note of any sort?"

"No. The police searched—" She shook her head. "So unlike him."

"I'll stay until you lock up and drive you home, Mrs. Clarke."

"Thank you, but I'm just down the street. I can walk."

"My car is right outside. Let me drive you home."

Mrs. Clarke nodded assent. "All right. I'll only be a minute."

She walked cursorily through the rooms, then came back. They left together and Mrs. Clarke locked the door.

* * *

"Come on in. I was just about to call you, Ski," Percy Davis said as Adam followed the former Police Sergeant into his small livingroom.

Whereas Adam's own livingroom seemed stuck somewhere around 1900, Percy's was definitely stuck somewhere around 1970. The walls were a dark wood paneling and the floor was carpeted with a gold shag rug. The furniture was big and bulky; there was a Hawaiian-cotton sofa along one wall and two tan vinyl recliners, side by side, a glass end-table between them with a tall wooden lamp on top. The recliners faced the most modern entry into the room, a huge flat-screen, high-definition television with speakers on either side of it. From his chair with the remote control, Percy could turn on the t.v., watch a DVD, or even listen to satellite radio. He called it his command center.

Percy settled into the recliner whose seat was nearly rump-spring and gestured Adam to the sofa. "Lt. Burke asked me to run a plate for you. Black van or SUV. Mass. License: 24R-*blank-blank-blank*. Right?"

"Right. What have you got?" Adam sat on the edge of the sofa.

"I've got several pages' worth."

"With names and addresses of owners?"

"By town, then owner." Percy drew a print out from the magazine rack on the floor next to his chair. "Here you go, knock yourself out."

Adam scanned down the list, looking for the addresses in Pittsley and Sipponet.

Percy pulled at a lever on the side of the chair and the footrest bounced up as he tilted back. "What's it all about, anyway?"

"Theft."

"Theft of what?" Percy crossed his legs at the ankles, prepared to settle in.

Adam didn't answer. He was staring at one of the names. *Joe Woods*. But Joe Woods was in jail. He'd been involved in the Nicole Fayette case, disposing of her body. But that wasn't why he was in prison. He was in jail, along with Marvel Kane, for trying to kill Julia when she was investigating Nicole's death.

"Can you find out if this vehicle has changed ownership?" Adam pointed to a license number.

"This list is current through September. It would have to have changed within the past couple of days. But how likely is that?"

"Not very, I suppose. More likely that someone else is just using it."

"Who's it belong to?"

"Joe Woods."

"Oh, that scumbag. He's where he belongs. So if that's the van, it had to be somebody else driving it. Didn't he work for Ellis Chalmers? Maybe Ellis knows something."

"I'll ask him."

"Ellis is pretty tight-lipped."

"Meaning?"

"Maybe I should go along with you?" Suddenly there was an eagerness in his voice.

"He lives in Sipponet. You think he's going to talk to a retired Pittsley cop?"

"He might. Or maybe his Mrs. will. Evie and I went to school together."

"Okay, let's give it a shot."

"Now?" Percy's face brightened.

Adam gestured him up and Percy pushed down the footrest and hurled himself out of his favorite chair.

Ellis Chalmers' farm was one of the largest produce farms in Sipponet, but his specialty was Macomber turnips. These were an historically southeastern Massachusetts vegetable, hybridized by two brothers in Westport in the 19th century. The hybrid—a cross between a turnip, rutabaga, cabbage, and radish—is the sweetest white turnip known and a favorite among people who find the yellow variety too harsh and pungent. Harvesting would come after the first deep frost, and it stored well through the winter. Not yet as famous as the Vidalia onion, but the Macomber turnip had made it into the New York Times recipe section several years back and sales had boomed. Turnips and butternut squash were his cash crops in the autumn and the farmhands were tending the vines.

Evie Chalmers greeted them at the screen door and stepped out onto the porch. "Percy Davis. How nice to see you. It's been a long time. How the hell are you?"

Evie Chalmers was a little shorter than medium height and somewhat stocky. She didn't wear the traditional apron and long skirt or put her hair up in a bun. Did farm women do that anymore? Adam wondered. No, Evie wore faded jeans, scuffed boots, a green-and-black plaid flannel shirt, and had short steel-grey hair. Her only concession to femininity was lipstick. And although far from delicate, she had her nails manicured. Probably, Adam thought, to distinguish her calloused hands from her husband's.

"Doing fine, Evie. Nice to see you, too. Is Ellis about?"

She inclined her head to the side. "He's out in the field, somewhere but I don't know exactly where. Anything I can do?"

"Maybe so," Percy replied and indicated Adam. "This here's Adam Sabeski."

"How do you do? Come on in, I'm just making coffee." She turned and held the screen door open for them.

They followed her into the big country kitchen, directly off the hallway.

"Now sit down and have some coffee and pie."

"Thanks, Evie, but we won't take but a couple of minutes of your time."

"Nonsense. Don't think you're going to pop up after this long and not say a proper hello." She gestured to them to sit down at the table.

"We don't want to put you to any trouble, Evie."

"No trouble at all," she said as she went about pouring coffee from the pot on the stove. "Two things Ellis always wants when he gets back off the tractor—a big slice of pie and a cup of hot coffee. Me, I prefer tea. Just made some lemon tea. Which would your rather?"

Both men opted for coffee, which she poured into large white mugs. Then she placed a huge mounded apple pie on the table and alongside it a butternut squash pie. "One or the other?"

"Either is fine for me," said Percy.

"Same here," said Adam.

"Try them both." She cut a generous slice of each one for both of the men and added some fresh whipped cream for topping.

"So what are you doing with yourself these days, Percy?"

"I'm retired from the force now."

"Is that right? It goes by so damn fast, doesn't it? How's Lydia?"

"She's well. She still volunteers at the hospital consignment shop in Dartmouth and keeps me in tow." He pronounced it 'Dark-muf' like most of the locals. "How's your family?"

"Scattered all over the place. Sally's in Wareham and Carol's in Gloucester. We get to see them every now and again. I baby-sit Sally's two children once in a while. But Jacob is in Oregon and Eli is in Arizona. We were hoping one of the boys would take over the farm, but they both graduated college and went looking for jobs where they sweat less and earn more. You know how it is these days with farming."

She sat down with her own mug of tea.

"So, who's going to grow the Macombers after Ellis quits?" Percy asked.

"Are you kidding, Ellis quit? " she rolled her bright blue eyes. "But I suppose after we go the kids will sell the place one day and it'll become a housing development or an industrial park. It's a rotten shame, isn't it? But so goes the country."

"The pie is delicious, Mrs. Chalmers, thank you," said Adam.

"You're welcome. Call me Evie. I'm glad you like the pie. I use three different varieties of apples. We have an orchard down back. And the squash is home grown. So where are you from, Adam?"

"Pittsley."

"Are you on the police force, too?"

"No. I'm a veterinarian."

"Oh. Well, we don't have farm animals. Just a couple of barn cats. They're all fixed."

"Actually," Percy said. "we just came to find out about the van that Joe Woods had."

"Him? What a nasty bit of business he turned out to be. Never liked him. But Ellis let him live in the out-building because he worked hard and he showed up sober. You don't know how hard it is to find that combination anymore."

"Do you know what happened to his van?"

"Funny thing," she said pouring a stream of honey into her lemon tea. "It was here for a while. You know, after he went to prison. Then I believe he gave it to Dennis Buckley. Joe worked for him on weekends sometimes. I don't know if any money changed hands, but I did see Dennis driving it off the property. Why are you interested in it?"

"Just routine," Percy answered.

She grimaced. "You sound like Ellis when he doesn't want me to know we've got blight. You men are all like. Don't worry, I won't ask again."

They made small pleasantries as they finished their pie. Adam noted that everything was perfectly maintained. No wear spots in the linoleum. No drawer-pulls off the door or cabinets. The appliances were all new, including a state-of-the-art microwave and sundry countertop conveniences—Cuisinart, bread machine, blender, etc. And in fact the countertop was granite. All of it clearly suggested that the Chalmers were doing very well indeed.

"Drop in again, Percy," Evie said as they were ready to go. "After harvesting, Ellis is back to normal working hours. It was good to see you. Nice meeting you, Adam."

They thanked her again and left.

"What do you know about Dennis Buckley?" Percy asked as they got back into Adam's truck.

"I know he's got a construction company in Pittsley. Buckley Builders.

Successful, I hear. I see him around. Not exactly the type to be stealing calves and goats. Nor the sort that would need a second-hand van from Joe Woods. What do *you* know about him?"

"Nothing much. He doesn't have a sheet and he's never had any problems with the police. Want to go have a look-see anyway?"

"Sure. Why not?"

They found Dennis Buckley in the equipment yard of his company walking down a line of front-end loaders and bulldozers. By the empty spaces in between, Adam surmised most of the heavy equipment was out on jobs.

Buckley was tall and trim, with black hair and blue eyes. Handsome, by any standard. His clothes—designer jeans, boots, and a navy blue sweater over a light blue shirt—were, to Adam, a masquerade of country attire. All the elements were right, but his clothes were too new and expensive...and perfectly clean.

He seemed to know both Adam and Percy by sight. "Good morning, gentlemen. What can I do for you?"

"You could loan me a few of these suckers for my back yard," Percy said

"Anything for the constabulary." Buckley answered with a false smile.

Percy investigated a very new crawler, stroking the smooth yellow fender like the withers of a horse. "You drive these yourself?"

"Used to. My main transportation now is a Beemer, easier to park."

"I understand you have Joe Woods' van. You selling it? Adam here might be interested."

"What makes you think I have Joe's van?" He thrust his thumbs in his pockets and assumed a defiant posture.

"I was talking with Evie Chalmers. She happened to mention it. Is it for sale?"

"Not that I know of. I'm just holding it for him."

"It's going to be a helluva long time before he uses it again," Percy said, tearing himself away from the dozer, "if ever."

"I'm just doing him a favor by storing it."

"Mind if we have a look at it?"

Buckley hesitated only a second, but a strange look passed over his face. "It's in a garage I have off-site. I'll give Joe a message and if he wants to sell, I can arrange to have you look at it. It'll take a day or two." He turned to Adam. "But I don't think it's much of an upgrade from your truck there."

"I'm not looking to upgrade," Adam answered defensively. He was acutely aware that Dennis Buckley was several years younger than himself and some millions richer. "I just need something to transport animals. I can move a goat or calf easier in a van than a truck bed."

"Well, the van's at least ten years' old. Not in the best condition, either."

"All the better."

Buckley made an expression of indifference. "Whatever."

"Give me a call after you talk to Woods," Adam said. "I'm listed."

Neither he nor Percy said anything until they had driven off the property.

"What do you make of that?" Adam asked.

"Patronizing son-of-a-bitch, ain't he?"

"He certainly doesn't want us looking at that van. The question is, what's he likely to do about it?"

Percy shook his head. "I expect he'll leave it where it is. Pretend to contact Joe Woods and tell you it's not for sale."

"But," Adam continued, "he's also going to want to clean it out."

"Right you are. But why the hell would Buckley steal animals? He could buy a herd of them."

"We don't know that *he* did it. He might have let someone else use the van. But the question is a good one. That's what's been bothering me. I wondered why anybody would steal the animals when they could simply buy them? Of course they're not cheap. Good Saanens probably go for close to Two Hundred apiece. Belted Galways can go for a Thousand."

"And," Percy added, cop-like, "there'd be a paper trail. A check, a transaction, a bill-of-sale. Somebody would know."

"So maybe whoever took them doesn't want anybody to know they have them."

Percy shook his head. "I don't get it."

"Neither do I."

"So now what?"

Adam looked at the clock on the dashboard. "I've got to get back to my clinic. Pick me up around five in your car. I'm thinking he'll stay put until his equipment comes back. Then let's see where he goes after he closes up."

"May as well. I got nothing better to do."

Adam hid a smile. He knew Percy was loving this. As was he.

* * *

When Julia arrived home, she found Martin waiting for her in his car in her driveway. She let Cat into the backyard and proceeded into the house with the pastor trailing behind.

"You look like bad news," he commented as Julia led him into the livingroom.

She sat down in the armchair and didn't immediately offer any explanation. The last time Martin had been in her livingroom, she remembered, he had driven her home from Massachusetts General Hospital, where she'd been examined after nearly being killed by one of Nicole Fayette's murderers. Joe Woods, in fact. That was when Adam had come over to make up with her, and Martin ultimately realized that she really wasn't interested in him. She knew she had wounded him deeply.

"What's wrong?" Martin asked as he sat down in the wing chair across from her.

"The Reverend Chauncy is dead."

It took a minute to register. "Benjamin is dead?"

"When I got there this morning, the police had just left."

"The police? What happened?"

"He hung himself."

"What?!" Martin slumped back into his chair.

"I spoke with his housekeeper," Julia continued. "It must have happened last night."

He asked the same questions she had about whether Benjamin had been sick, or whether he'd left a note, and she gave him the same unsatisfying answers she'd been given.

After a silence he said, "It's my fault."

"Why your fault?"

"You were there, you heard me on the phone," he said abjectly, "I practically accused him of knowing something about the murders and Ponlok's disappearance."

"That's not what I heard."

"Not directly, Julia. But he could read between the lines."

"If that's true, the only reason he would react this way is if he did know something. Maybe that's why he took his own life."

"But if I hadn't—"

"Look, you're trying to help this boy. We both are. And if he was complicit in this somehow, that's his guilt not yours."

"And now we'll never know."

Julia rubbed her forehead. She felt the beginnings of a headache and she rarely ever got headaches. "We still have two more days."

"If we're right." Martin clasped hands together. "But I don't know what more to do."

Julia did not respond. She knew that that was said to a Higher Authority.

After Martin left, Julia heated up some canned chicken soup for herself and a kibble snack for Cat. Adam had called to say he wouldn't be over tonight. He was looking into the theft of the goat or goats with Percy. She was just as glad he wouldn't be there. She needed to think, to concentrate, but her head was pounding.

She took two aspirins and lay down on the couch with a book so she could pretend to herself she was reading while she tried to think about Ponlok. But her thoughts drifted instead to Tessa. She missed her so. She wanted to pick up the phone and call her friend and tell her about Adam, and Martin, about Ponlok, and about the decision she had to make about work. She wanted to say, "Come on, Tessa, let's take a ride down to Newport and watch all the rich people's boats and have a beer and a blooming onion at that cheesy restaurant on the water." And the two of them would drive off, chatting and singing all the way.

She wanted to hear Tessa laugh with that wide mouth too large for her face and talk passionately about her music, and she wanted to hear Tessa's enthusiasm when she told Julia where she and Billy and B.J. were going to perform next weekend and make Julia promise to be there.

Tessa, Billy, and B.J. had their own band. They were the *Foot Stompin' Jug Band* (with B.J. on jug) or *Mozart Street* (classical with a party beat), depending on the occasion. Billy played cello and fiddle, and tutored private students in their home. Tessa had played guitar, banjo, and mandolin, and taught in the regional high school. But after Tessa died, Billy gave up the band. There would be no more performances to go to.

Tears came to her eyes as she thought about the funeral when all of Tessa's students for the past twenty years came to pay her tribute by playing Tessa's own composition, "New England Overture." B.J. and his father orchestrated the piece, B.J. played the violin and Billy conducted. She tried to hear the music in her mind. But before she realized what was happening, she was asleep.

* * *

Percy's old black Ford idled in front of Adam's house less than a minute before he came out. Neither man was in a talkative mood as they drove the back roads to Buckley Builders. It was always that way when they were working together. They'd know each other long enough that there was no necessity to talk.

Percy parked down from the gate and out of view at the curve of the road.

After a little while longer in silence, Percy finally said, "I'm thinking we should split up after he leaves. Why don't I go inside his compound from the rear and see if the van is stored back there? He could have been lying to us about keeping it off-site. You can follow Buckley in my car."

"Don't you think he'll have surveillance cameras and motion lights in there?"

"Of course he will. But I haven't been a cop all these years for nothing. Remember when we used to go after poachers?"

"All too well." He and Percy had spent countless nights in tracking down and catching hunters out of season. They had even done a few dogfight and cockfight raids together. Percy was as stealthy as any criminal.

"I can actually walk to my house from here," Percy said. "Just come back there after you're done and I'll drive you home."

As they sat watching as truck after truck of the workers began leaving the construction yard. Then nothing. Then they saw the gunmetal-gray BMW pull out. Percy immediately left his car and Adam slid over behind the wheel. Buckley got out, closed and padlocked the gate behind him, then drove off. Percy was already out of sight as Adam slowly followed the BMW at a practiced distance.

Adam expected his quarry to go to either of two places in Pittsley—to his off-site garage, or to his home. But Buckley did neither.

It wasn't long before Adam realized that the BMW was leaving Pittsley and headed for Sipponet Village. Was that where his off-site storage was located? That made sense. Even though Dennis Buckley lived and worked in Pittsley now, he grew up in Sipponet.

The BMW traveled down Arbor Street towards the Village Green, then circled half-way around the Green and pulled into the driveway of a large, imposing Colonial-style house. Adam watched in his rear-view mirror as he drove past the house.

Buckley got out and went up to the front door. Adam knew that house. It belonged to Usha Kane, the former Mayor. His son, Marvel, had lived on the green, too. He knew that house even better, because that's where he almost beat Marvel into the ground when he was searching for Julia. He might have killed the little weasel if he hadn't told him that Joe Woods had taken her out on his boat to dump overboard. They never convicted Marvel for killing Nicole Fayette but at least they got him for conspiracy to commit murder—Julia's.

Marvel Kane, Joe Woods, and Dennis Buckley had all run together as kids. They stayed tight friends over the years. But what did that have to do with Marvel's father?

Adam waited where he could see both the front and the back of the house. If Buckley came out the back way to go to the van, he would know.

But no one came out. Ten minutes. Twenty minutes. Half and hour passed and there was no activity.

He should have gotten a coffee to stay awake. He was tired, and spending nights with Julia didn't exactly afford him a full night's sleep. He shook his head. She'd stunned him this morning by bringing up the 'm' word. Marriage wasn't something he had ever seriously considered. Where was this going with them? He'd always believed he'd be alone all his life. But was that a preference or just a default position? He'd never actually had to contemplate it before. None of his romantic relationships had progressed this far before. He'd been quite sure he'd wind up like Goody, independent and cantankerous. The fact was, he thought he'd make a lousy husband.

What was the matter with him that he seemed unable to do what came so easily to so many others? Was he too practical? Too cynical? Too realistic? Maybe it took a kind of idealism to think that there was such a thing as lasting love. Maybe any idealism he might have had or wanted to have, got lost along the way. Lost along a booby-trapped trail in the seventh circle of hell. But that was a long-ago hell that had since been replaced by the war in Iraq. And that made him feel a lot like Percy…an old warhorse with outdated memories and emotions.

Finally, after about thirty-five minutes, Dennis Buckley came out the front door, got back into his car and drove off.

Adam was in a dilemma. Should he follow Buckley, or wait to see if Usha Kane came out? He decided to follow Buckley.

Wrong choice.

He mentally kicked himself as he arrived at Buckley's house back in Pittsley. Buckley simply pulled his car into the driveway and went inside.

Should he go back to Usha's house? He'd already lost about fifteen minutes by following Buckley home and it would be another fifteen minutes back. Adam looked at his watch. It was only a quarter after six.

What the hell, he thought, I may as well find out whatever I can.

When he arrived back at Usha Kane's house, there was a white F350 pick-up truck in the driveway where Buckley's Beemer had been. On the door panel was a logo with black lettering circling it. Adam did not have to get any closer to see it. He knew that logo. Everyone around there did. It was a tipped basket of vegetables showing potatoes, carrots, corn, and turnips. The name around the basket would read Chalmer's Farm, Sipponet, MA.

Finally, the front door opened. Evie Chalmers stepped out, said something to the man in the doorway, Usha Kane, and walked back to the truck.

Oh, well, Adam thought, that explains it. Evie had probably delivered a produce order to Usha or his wife. He watched as the pick-up backed out of the driveway and drove off in the direction of the farm.

He wished he had his pipe with him. He rarely smoked it anymore. But at times like these, when he just wanted to sit and think, he liked having the stem between his teeth, his hand on the warm bowl. The smell of latttaquie in the tobacco mix was soothing. It helped him concentrate.

Just as he was going to start the motor, another pick-up truck pulled into Usha's driveway. Black. Old. No logo or lettering on the door panel.

Adam didn't recognize the truck. But he did recognize the driver when he emerged from the cab. Bob Carriou. Pittsley selectman Al Carriou's brother. Partner with Dennis Buckley. Could Usha be involved Parkwood Development business? There was no mention of it by Kip. It must be something else. Probably nothing more to find out here, he supposed. He may as well drive back to Percy's house to see what his friend discovered.

"I didn't find Joe's van, did you?" Percy asked from his command center as Adam entered the livingroom.

"Nope," Adam replied, sitting on the sofa. Then he told Percy about the evening's dance card. "And Evie Chalmers. But I figured she was just delivering a produce order."

"They don't deliver."

"But for the former Mayor—?"

"They don't deliver."

Adam took that in along with Percy's thoughtful look. "You can't be thinking Evie's connected to all this."

"I don't automatically think she's not. Just because I know her. Just because she's a woman. Or just because she gave us pie."

Percy's wife, Lydia, was passing through the hallway with a green plastic tub of laundry when she stopped and backed up. Backing up was not Lydia's best angle, as she'd put on a few pounds over the years. But she was still a pretty woman with fine features, clear blue eyes, and natural curly blonde hair that she kept almost natural these days with a little chemical help.

"Who gave you pie?"

"Evie Chalmers."

"Oh. Her. What were you doing at Evie Chalmers'?"

"Adam and I went out to ask a few questions. That's all."

"Oh." She lifted her chin just a little and continued on.

Percy shook his head at Adam. "I'm going to hear about this later."

"Why?"

"I dated Evie in high school. Before I started dating Lydia."

Adam chuckled. "High school?"

"I know. A lifetime ago. But to Lydia…." He sighed.

Adam laughed. "I think its kind of sweet that she still gets jealous after all these years."

"Sweet, my patoutie. Now I'm going to get the third-degree. 'What kind of pie? How does she look? What did she say? Is she a good baker? How does she *look*?' And then I'm going to have to 'comfort' her tonight and take her out to dinner tomorrow."

Adam laughed even more heartily. "You wolf."

Percy smiled in embarrassment and the color rose in his cheeks. Over the sound of the washing machine in the laundry room, he said, "Speaking of that," he grumbled, "how's Julia?"

"She's fine. She's still trying to decide whether she wants to go into private practice or not."

"You've been together a couple of years now."

"About that." Adam became instinctively wary. He had a feeling he knew what was coming.

"Going to marry her?" Percy looked him sideways.

"I was waiting for that. You're the second person to ask me that question today."

"Who was the first?"

"Julia."

"Oh-h-h." Percy grinned. "So it's at that point, is it? What did you say?"

"I basically said I don't know."

Now it was Percy's turn to laugh. "Which, to any woman, means 'no.' How'd she take it?"

"She seemed fine. I think she understands."

"Understands what?"

"That we're together and all, but I don't exactly want to live with her."

"You've got stones, I'll give you that."

"You said *what* to Julia?" Lydia stopped mid-way in the hall on her way back to the kitchen.

Adam had known Lydia as long as he'd known Percy, and he liked her. She was forthright and never reluctant to speak her mind. But he wished her timing had been off. There was no avoiding her now.

"Julia said she couldn't see us living together. And I kind of agreed."

"You agreed?" Lydia said accusingly.

"Yes."

"Adam Sabeski, you are such an ass."

Adam lifted out his hands helplessly. "What was I supposed to say? I was being truthful."

Lydia shook her head. "Tell him, Percy." She marched on towards the kitchen shaking her head.

Adam looked at Percy askance.

Percy swiped his hands in front of his face in a gesture of 'I do not want to get into this.'

* * *

Ponlok sat on the mattress on the floor, legs crossed. He could not hear anything outside. No cars passing by, no night insects, no owls, just silence. They had given him a ham and cheese sandwich, an apple, and a glass of milk a little while ago, so he estimated it was the evening of the fifth day of his captivity. He knew it was evening because of the sandwich. It was always cereal for breakfast, soup for lunch, and a sandwich for supper. It was always two men, one taller and one shorter, both hooded. The taller man always stayed in the doorway to prevent him from running out. The shorter one gave him the food and took out his slop bucket at breakfast and at supper, replacing it with a clean white plastic bucket each time. But they never spoke to him, not even when he asked why he was there.

His mother must be worried. Or had she already given him up for dead? But he wasn't dead and he didn't know why they were keeping him alive. For what? Perhaps he would be sold for the sex trade. What else could it be? There was no way to escape from this room, but perhaps if they moved him—

He heard a series of footsteps outside his door and a shuffling as though there was a group of people. Then quiet. Then a voice he'd heard before, a man's voice full of emotion, an orator, spoke:

'*We are witness to Armageddon. The End Days have begun. It is the final battle of Good and Evil. Good shall prevail. But it will be a mighty fight and it will destroy the City of Joy, Jerusalem, the city which God has chosen to put His name there—1 Kings 11:36, 1 Kings 14:21—2] And I John saw the holy city, new Jerusalem, coming down from God out of heaven, prepared as a bride adorned for her husband. And God said—Revelation 21:6-8—'I am Alpha and Omega, the beginning and the end. I will give unto him that is athirst of the fountain of the water of life freely. He that overcometh shall inherit all things; and I will be his God, and he shall be my son. But the fearful, and unbelieving, and the abominable, and murderers, and whoremongers, and sorcerers, and idolaters, and all liars, shall have their part in the lake which burneth with fire and brimstone: which is the second death. to make way for a New Jerusalem and a new era.*'

"*Today,*" *the voice continued,* "*we are one day closer to Eternity, O Jerusalem.*"

"*O Jerusalem,*" *repeated a chorus of voices.*

Ponlok had never heard of Jerusalem. Without television or radio and only a rudimentary understanding of English, his apartment-mates came home from their hard day's labor, ate their meager meal of rice and vegetables, paid their respects to Buddha, and went to bed. What was this Army of Gedon? Had a war begun since he was kidnapped? Did it have anything to do with why he was here? The voice went on but the words were meaningless to Ponlok.

"*Only the penitent shall be saved. What we do here is ordained of God from the Beginning.*

"*God is mortally displeased with Mankind. He has expressed his wrath since the beginning of Biblical history and wiped clear the earth of sinners. Each time He allowed us to begin again. But He has run out of patience. These are the End Times.*

"*Never has humankind fallen farther from His Word, from our Covenant with Him. We have never been more Evil. There is no longer any doubt that we are in Satan's thrall. In his grasp, earth is but a ball of clay that he will crush between his talons.*

"*Only God can help us now. But we are not worthy. Look at us!*"

Ponlok could hear footsteps pacing.

"*Look what we humans have done! Turn on your televisions to any news station and you will see it. Read any newspaper. Any news magazine. Any radio broadcast. Any Internet news. All over the globe, atrocities are committed that would shame the worst barbarians. We kill wantonly, mutilate, slaughter, maim. We take pleasure in it. We pollute, defile, befoul our own nest. We are addicted to drugs, to sex, to violence, to everything vile. Lying, stealing, cheating—these aren't even considered punishable anymore.*

"*We are hurtling towards our Doom. God has not accepted our sacrifices, fellow Guardians. Why? I have prayed upon it. Why is God not appeased by our sacrifices?*

"*I believe it is because we did not treat the bodies of the Young with respect. We have given them over to men who defiled them. That cannot happen again.*

"*This time, we will purify the body after the sacrifice. That was our mistake and now we have a chance to rectify it. We will perform the ceremony in the right way, at the right time, with the right regard, and God will take heed and forgive us our trespasses. This is our Duty for the world of the elect. Amen.*"

"*Amen,*" *echoed the others.*

Friday, October 6th

He hadn't gone to Julia's last night. He phoned to say he was working with Percy, which was true and not true. He was with Percy, true, but he was not really working. After scolding him royally, Lydia made him stay for supper and afterwards he and Percy knocked back a few beers and they both dozed off in front of the t.v. until, around midnight, Lydia finally insisted that her husband come to bed and Adam go home.

That was the thing about not being married. He didn't have to be accountable for his time and nobody could tell him to come to bed because it was getting late, not if he didn't want to.

In his clinic office that morning, Adam listened as Kip told him over the phone that he and Terri had worked through the night after Adam had called to ask whether Usha Kane had any involvement in the Parkwood Development Corporation—well, not straight through the night, Kip said—they'd taken breaks—well, two long breaks—two was the best he could manage these days.

"You're getting old, Kip."

"I'm also getting married."

"What?" Adam was completely taken aback. "As of when?"

"I proposed last night, and she said yes."

Terri, he knew, had moved into Kip's Commonwealth Avenue condo eight months ago after a two-year office relationship. She decided to go to law school and he encouraged it. She was smart and an absolute bulldog on details. One day, he fully expected to make her partner. At first Kip told him it was going to be Kipper and Tavares.

"Well...congratulations!" Adam recovered. "When's the wedding?"

"Probably not until she graduates."

Adam rolled his eyes grateful that Kip couldn't see him. "So, Kipper and Kipper attorneys-at-law?"

"Looks like it."

"I owe you both an engagement present."

"You bet your ass you do. Something really expensive," Kip joked. "But now for the bad news."

Even with all their due diligence, Kip said, they found no evidence of any legal relationship between Usha Kane and Parkwood Development. If there was one, it was too well hidden and he didn't want to spend any more of Amos' money on it.

Adam understood that Kip worked on billable hours and he respected his friend for trying to keep the fee down for his client. But Adam wasn't satisfied with ending it.

"I'm going to have a crack at the Selectmen again, Kip, tell me what to say."

He sensed Kip's reticence. Maybe his friend didn't think he was capable of handling this. Maybe he was right. Adam and Kip had grown up together, gone to 'Nam together, came back and went to Tufts University together. Afterwards, he went to Harvard Law and Adam stayed at Tufts Veterinary School. They had been so alike in the beginning. But Adam had a different experience in 'Nam than he did. Not that they talked about it. They never did. But Kip obviously saw the change in him when they got back. Kip had stayed on track; Adam got off the train somewhere.

Adam knew Kip wondered why he remained in Pittsley even though he could well be at Boston's Angell Memorial Animal Hospital, one of the largest and most renowned animal hospitals in the world; its technology and caliber of staff rivaled most human hospitals. If Kip were a veterinarian, that's what he'd choose. But Adam liked being a country vet. That's where they differed.

Kip had once told Adam he used to worry about him. His mood swings. The fact that he sometimes disappeared for days into the woods backpacking. He told Adam he'd become too solitary, that he'd turn into an old recluse like Goody. Then came Julia. Sometimes, Kip had said, just having someone else to think about, to care about, changes everything.

Not that Kip had been all that successful in his personal life. He was divorced from Danielle a long time before meeting Terri. He'd gone through his share of unfulfilling relationships by then. Purely his fault, he acknowledged. He'd vowed to get his head straight before he started dating again. For the first year that Terri worked for him, he hardly made eye contact.

"She thought I had Asperger's," Kip told him, "or some other medical problem."

When he finally did start looking at her, he realized he liked what he saw. Not just that she was attractive, and she was that, but that she was bright and funny and reliable, and she was nice. Whatever one might say about his ex-wife—beautiful, gifted, ambitious—no one would ever say 'nice.' Not-nice women used to fascinate him. But nice was something he'd come to value. A much underrated quality. Adam had agreed.

"I'm going to pursue this, Kip. So tell me what to do," Adam insisted.

Although the chairman, Albert Carriou, wasn't there today, Madison Wentworth was. Madison was the oldest member of the Board of Selectman, and the only lawyer. Mostly insurance cases and workers comp. Ambulance chaser, Adam categorized him. Retired.

Like Carriou, Madison was a big beefy man who should have been smoking a big beefy cigar—which he was wont to do at every opportunity, however not in the town offices.

They shook hands cordially.

"Let's step outside back so I can light up," Madison said as he headed for the door.

Outside, the autumn air had a sunny chill to it. The woods behind the town hall were at the peak of their color. Blue jays screeched their squeaky-door call from the treetops and beyond. Adam missed the caw of crows that used to be so frequent, but their numbers had declined from

West Nile disease. He could hear crickets but couldn't pinpoint where they were coming from. He longed to spend time alone again in the wild.

As he sat on the stairs out of public view, Madison struck a match and put it to his cigar, saying, "Pretty soon, this'll be illegal, too."

"I hear it is, in some places," Adam commented.

"I know. It's a bitch, ain't it? You get to wondering what else they're going to make illegal. Probably obesity. Then I'll really be screwed. So what's this about, more eminent domain stuff?"

"Max Kipper thought he might go for an injunction," Adam said lazily.

"Bull shit. He should know better. And I'm insulted that he thinks I could be bluffed. Eminent domain is settled law. Federal law trumps district courts. What else's he got?"

"Parkwood Development Corporation."

Madison took a puff of cigar and watched it blow back into the breeze. "Go on."

"Conny Cranshaw. Dennis Buckley. Bob Carriou."

Madison's eye flicked.

"You didn't know."

Madison shrugged. "Doesn't matter. Everyone's entitled to their scoop in the pot."

"Are they? The brother of the chairman of the Board of Selectmen?"

"We are not our brothers' keepers." Madison took another puff of cigar. "Is that all?"

"Those are his show cards."

Madison looked at Adam keenly. "What're you doing here, shilling for Maxwell Kipper?"

"I live here. He doesn't. I care about this town."

Madison looked upward and paused. Then he looked back at Adam, his eyes unblinking. "Believe it or not, we thought very hard about these plans. We looked very carefully into that eminent domain decision in Connecticut. And we are convinced it will benefit the community."

"Which community? Not the bog men. Not the Juckets."

"You know the old saying, 'you can't make an omelet without breaking eggs.'"

Adam wanted to tell him where he could stick his omelet, but he wasn't about to lose control of the situation.

"Sorry, son," Madison concluded, "but I believe you've got squat with this."

Madison was only about fifteen years older than Adam, and he resented the selectman's paternalism. "Well, I guess we'll find out, won't we? In court."

"Like I said, this is settled law. How're you going to get to court?"

"By truck."

The selectman looked puzzled but Adam simply said a polite goodbye, leaving Madison Wentworth on the steps with his cigar half-smoked. Adam thought pleasurably that the selectman would soon find out how truthful he'd been.

His next stop would be to visit Conny Cranshaw. He and Conny were never on the best of terms, but he was hoping he could provoke the volatile man in revealing something. Of all of them, Conny was the loose cannon.

Cranland Trucking was on the other side of town. Conny managed both his trucking business and his development corporation—not Parkwood, by name, but Cranland Realty—out of a trailer office. Low overhead, Adam thought, not like Kip's overpriced offices. But Conny played in a sandbox where Kip, by comparison, played in a four-star athletic club, with martini bar.

Nonetheless, he had to acknowledge that Conny was a multimillionaire in that sandbox and he, Adam, couldn't come near it. So how was he going to play this?

"Sabeski," Conny greeted him, "friend of the dog and cat. Sorry, no takers here."

"I'm not here on animal business. I'm doing a favor for a friend."

"And who would that be?"

"Max Kipper."

Conny put his feet up on his desk. New shoes, brogans, Adam noticed. But short bandy legs, which is why he remained seated.

"I hear he rarely leaves Bean Town, guess they were right. What's he want from me?"

Few people other than sportscasters still said Bean Town, but Adam didn't comment. One thing he knew about Conny Cranshaw, he liked to hear himself talk. Maybe he should just let him.

"Confirmation, that's all," Adam answered.

"I heard he was hired by Amos Hall, that right?"

"That's right."

"To do with the eminent domain order. Well, that's closing the barn door after the horse is gone, isn't it?"

Conny gave him the kind of sneer Adam would have liked to remove, but he restrained himself and decided to dive in. "Kip is interested because you're involved in the development corporation that's going to get all that land."

Conny swung his feet down and leaned forward on his elbows towards Adam. "Who says?"

"Public record. Just how much do you expect to make on this deal?"

"None of your damn business."

Adam went on as if Conny hadn't answered. "'Cause it's going to take a ton of money to do the site work, the engineering, the building, managing the facility, staffing it, advertising. I'm thinking about ten million?"

Conny glared at him, then sneered again. "Try fifty. You got to spend money to make money."

"And you can't make an omelet without breaking eggs, right?" Walking clichés, all of them, Adam thought.

Conny looked baffled.

"But," Adam continued, "what I don't get is what Bob Carriou is doing on the list. You, and Buckley are the money people. Bob, now, he hasn't got any, does he? What's he bring to the table? His brother?" Connie stared at him and said nothing. "But then, I suppose Usha Kane has the real connections. Does he add treasure as well as talent to the company?"

"You've got your facts wrong," Conny replied snidely. "Usha Kane has nothing to do with it."

"What about the Chalmers?"

"I got nothing more to say to you. Except get outa here."

Adam got up to leave, saying, "Okay, Conny. As always, it's been nice talking to you. Thanks for your hospitality."

"Screw you, Jucket," Conny shouted after him.

* * *

Sam poked his head into Julia's office and tapped on the door.

She motioned him in. "Good morning, Sam."

He indicated the chair in front of her desk. "May I?"

"Of course."

He took the seat on the opposite side of the desk. "How are you this morning?" he asked.

"I'm well, thank you, and you?"

"Well, also." He crossed his legs.

No matter what the situation, Sam always observed the pleasantries. She had never known him to be anything but polite, formal, and fastidious. Today, he wore his white lab coat over his Oxford blue shirt and tan slacks with, of all things, a blazing red silk tie with birds on it. Different breeds, perching and flying, birds and more birds in all colors and combinations. She didn't know he liked birds. She didn't know very much at all, she realized, about Dr. Shing Wu. She'd met his wife twice at staff parties but Mai Wa did not speak much English. No, she did not know very much about her boss other than he took a mentor's interest in her, the fact that he was several years younger notwithstanding.

"Ray Alonzo called me at home last night."

She raised her eyebrow. "How'd he take it?"

"Like a bridegroom stranded at the altar."

"That bad?"

"At first. Then after we talked for a while he cheered up."

"Good. What did you say to him?"

"That I would take your place."

Julia reacted as though he'd told her he'd decided to become a ballet dancer.

"I didn't think you—" She took a deep breath. "Are you serious?" She shook her head. "Of course you're serious. You would never—but what made you decide that? When is this all going to happen?"

Sam placed his fingertips together. "I've resigned as of December 31st. That's ample time for them to find a replacement."

"But why?" She couldn't imagine it.

"New challenges. I've had an offer to teach part-time come the January semester and private practice gives me more flexibility to do that. So I'm going to accept."

"Teach where?"

"My *alma mater*, Harvard Medical. As an adjunct professor."

Julia smiled ruefully. "How is it that I take weeks to angst over a decision whether to change directions, and you do it practically overnight?"

"Do you really need me to answer that?"

"No. It's because I'm still uncertain of myself, I suppose."

"Which boils down to what?" he pressed.

"Fear."

Sam shook his head. "After all you've been through these past couple of years, do you still want to hang on to that fiction?"

He was right, of course. Sam was usually right—except for that one time when she felt he hadn't stuck up for her after the Superintendent dismissed her from Nicole's case. Then what did she do? She'd confronted the Superintendent, risked her job, and did what she had to do and didn't consider whether or not she was afraid.

And hadn't she picked herself up after her divorce from Phillip and changed jobs, changed locations, and started a new life? And hadn't she defended herself by attacking Joe Woods before he could attack her? In fact, when it came right down to it, she overcame her fears without hardly thinking about it.

"You're right, Sam. As almost always." She couldn't help needling him about his one lapse with her. "I'm too old to still be playing the timid ingénue. I'm a grandmother." She raised her index finger for emphasis. "A very *young* grandmother."

They went on to talk about her caseload, she indicating certain patients who would require medication that, not being an M.D. as he was, she was not licensed to prescribe. He agreed with her on every call she made. Since she would see Esther Davenport again right after their meeting, they strategized what to do about her.

Esther looked almost catatonic. She slouched in the chair facing Julia but looked beyond her hardly blinking. Her mouth was slack and her face seemed to sag.

"How are you feeling today, Esther?"

If that wasn't the dumbest question, I don't know what is, Julia thought. But she asked it purely to get her patient to say something.

"Esther?"

"Fine," Esther finally replied hollowly.

"You don't seem fine. What's wrong?" Julia waited a beat then said again, "What's wrong Esther?"

Esther pulled her eyes back from wherever she was looking and focused on Julia.

"Talk to me, Esther, what are you thinking about?"

"The end of everything," Esther said lugubriously.

Julia decided to try a new tactic. "Who's telling you this blarney, Esther? You said the other day that 'it is known.' But I don't know it. Dr. Sam doesn't know it. How is it that you know it and no one else does?"

Esther was jarred into the present. "I'm not the only one," she replied. "My brother knows it. My brother-in-law Ellis knows it, his wife Evie knows it, my husband Donald knows it."

"How?" This was the first time Esther had mentioned her family and Julia had not heard their names before. It was a good start. "How do they know it?"

"Because he told us. He said it's going to happen tomorrow night."

"Everything is going to end tomorrow night?" Julia quickly wrote 'suicide watch' in her notes. "Did God tell you this?"

"God doesn't speak to me. He speaks to Usha."

Julia felt a wave of cold air sweep over her. There could only be one Usha. The name was too uncommon. "Are you referring to Usha Kane?"

"Yes."

"How do you know him?" She had to repeat the question before Esther answered.

"He's my sister's husband. We we're three sisters." She counted on her fingers. "Evie married Ellis. Eileen married Usha. And I married Ellis' cousin."

Esther lived in Taunton so Julia had never thought of any Pittsley connections. She didn't know of an Evie and Ellis but there were so many marital interrelationships in this region, you never knew who was related to whom. It was more like a family cobweb than a family tree. If she'd known her patient was an in-law to the father of Marvel Kane, the man who tried to kill her, she would have withdrawn from the case on principle. She would have to now, in any event. She would let Sam know that he should probably take over the case. But as long as the session wasn't over yet, Julia decided to continue.

"So Usha Kane has told you that God told him the world is going to end tomorrow?"

"Tomorrow night."

"And," Julia decided to take a leap, "is Usha Kane one of the 'certain people' you mentioned who are trying to prevent this from happening?"

Esther shifted her gaze away from Julia again and did not answer.

"Esther?"

Her patient did not acknowledge.

"You haven't answered me."

But Esther was once again detached from the present. There was little point in continuing until they adjusted her meds, Julia decided.

"Do you want to go back to the ward now?"

Esther nodded in slow motion. Julia buzzed for the attendant.

As her patient was escorted out of the office, she turned as she reached the doorway.

"Goodbye, Dr. Arnault," she said with somber finality.

* * *

Adam sat in Billy's livingroom while B.J. was at the diningroom table doing homework. Billy had moved Tessa's chair, with her guitar on it, to the corner of the room. It used to be that she would sit there with B.J., checking his answers. Adam wondered how B.J. was doing in school as he watched the boy concentrate so hard his face was lowered over the page in the book. He was a good-looking boy, taller than his father now, but with most of Billy's features except for his mother's mouth that fit his face much better than it had hers. It was a hard time for both of them since

Tessa died, but they were lucky to have each other. Billy was a good father and B.J. was growing into a fine young man.

"So everything's ready for tonight?" Billy asked.

"All ready," Adam answered. "We'll get the detours in first. Then the Juckets will alternate with the bog trucks. It's got to get done fast."

"You really think they can do this without getting caught?"

"I'm less worried about getting caught than getting stopped."

Billy rubbed the back of his neck. "I try not to think so much about the things I can't see. But what I would give to see this, even for just a few seconds. It's going to be something, Adam, isn't it?"

"I do believe it will get their attention."

They never really discussed the fact that Billy was blind or whether he had any visual memories. Adam's sight was so keen and his aim so accurate, he could identify a red-shouldered hawk from a Cooper's from two hundred feet without binoculars. He'd always felt that his extraordinary vision defined him and he regretted that his friend couldn't witness what they would accomplish.

"Excuse me, Adam," B.J. said from the next room.

"What is it, B.J.?"

"I was just wondering if there was any news about Ponlok. Have you heard anything"

"No, I'm afraid not. It's in the hands of the State Police now."

Billy cocked his head towards his son and Adam saw his expression change from eager to parental. "It's definitely an abduction, is it, Adam? They don't think it might have been some sort of accident? Or a runaway?"

"They don't think so." There was no reason for him to run away; they had looked into that. And if it were an accident, there'd be some kind of trace. They had stopped searching the woods.

"Terrible thing," Billy said, "a child being snatched up like that, and then gone. Maybe forever. For what?"

"I don't know," Adam said. But it wasn't for ransom. Was it for sex? He did not see any reason to mention it.

"Adam?" B.J. said again, lifting up his head from his book. "Did you find that black van? The one Dr. Arnault told you about that took the goat?"

He had shared that information with Billy, who obviously had told his son. "Not yet, B.J., but we're looking."

"I saw a black van when I was working at the bog."

"I'm sure there are a lot of black vans."

"Did it have a bumpersticker?"

"Julia didn't mention a bumpersticker. What kind of bumpersticker?"

"A white sticker with black lettering that said, 'Cape Cod Tunnel.'" Of course, there was no such thing. It was meant as a joke on outsiders. "Really lame," B.J. pronounced.

It probably wasn't the same one, Adam thought, but he should confirm it with Julia. It was remotely possible that she had overlooked it. "Mind if I use your phone, Billy? I just want to double-check that with Julia."

Billy pointed to the stationery phone on the end table and Adam dialed Julia's office. The line was busy so he hung up.

"Did you see anybody around the van, Beej?"

"No. Sorry. Are you going to look for the goat?"

"That goat and others, and some calves that were taken."

"When are you going?"

"Tomorrow or the next day, I suppose, why?"

B.J. put down his pencil. "Could I go with you?"

"For what reason?"

"Because somebody killed my calf a couple of years ago and they never found out who. I'd just like to know if it's the same person."

"I don't think it would be such a good idea for you to go with me."

Billy lowered his voice as he said, "Maybe it would, Adam. I can think of a hundred reasons not to involve B.J. and just one to take him along: he needs something to do. He's been really upset about Ponlok. Maybe this would help him feel useful. As long as it wasn't dangerous. He could just come along for the ride, couldn't he?"

"Sure," Adam agreed. "It won't be dangerous. I'll keep him in the truck." He turned to B.J. "Your dad just convinced me to let you ride shotgun, Beej."

B.J. smiled broadly. "Thanks, Adam. Thank, Dad."

* * *

After leaving a message with Sam about Esther's meds, Julia phoned the State Police. Very shortly, a gruff masculine voice identified himself at John McDermott.

"Lt. McDermott? This is Dr. Julia Arnault. Do you remember me?"

"Of course. The Nicole Fayette case."

She immediately envisioned the Lieutenant as she'd seen him two years ago.

He had been the investigator in charge when Nicole's body was discovered twenty years previously. He could never let go of the case, but could never resolve it until Julia stirred it up again and nearly got killed in the process. She had visited him in his office after Nicole's daughter, Sherry, had become her patient. He was just as terse now as he had been then. He had reminded her of an aged Dudley Do-Right—with a spare frame, buzz-cut grey hair, and a long thin face with a square jaw. She would bet that he hadn't changed an iota.

"I thought you were going to retire, Lieutenant."

"Guess I'm not ready to hang it up yet. What can I do for you?"

"Were you aware that another child has disappeared in Pittsley?"

He paused just briefly enough for Julia to sense concern.

"No."

"When I learned the matter was in the hands of the State Police, I thought you might be involved."

"No. I'm administrative now, not a field officer."

"I believe it may be the same cult, Lieutenant."

He said nothing, so she filled him in on everything she knew about Ponlok's disappearance.

"And," she added, "we think...that is, Reverend Ryman and I think some ritual is going to occur tomorrow night. Which doesn't give us much time."

He remained silent.

"Can you do anything to help us?"

"Not officially."

"But you must have your suspicions about who's in the cult. Can't you check them out or something?"

"Call me at home tonight. Around seven." He gave his telephone number.

"There's something else I wanted to ask you." She was going to quiz him about investigative psychologists working with the police, then decided against it. "Never mind," she said, "it can wait."

She wondered if she should call Martin. But there wasn't anything to report, really. Perhaps after she spoke with McDermott tonight.

It seemed as though seven o'clock would never come and she couldn't wait any longer. Julia dialed Lt. McDermott's home at six-fifty and waited as the phone rang. The answering machine went on with its impersonal automated voice, so she hung up.

After ten minutes more, she dialed again. He picked up on the third ring.

"Lieutenant? Julia Arnault."

"Yes."

"I believe you had something to tell me?" Every time she talked with him, she found herself adopting his short, nearly monosyllabic speech.

"I don't have any answers for you, Dr. Arnault. Only a suspicion."

"Which is?"

"Usha Kane. Marvel's father."

There was that name again. Did all roads lead to Usha? "You think he has something to do with this?"

"I think he did a good job of protecting his son for twenty years. He has a lot of connections and no small amount of influence. Or at least he did until Marvel went to jail. I don't know what, if any, political relation he has to the new mayor."

"But what makes you think he's involved with the cult."

"My gut."

His gut might just be right, she thought, but declined to tell him about Esther for confidentiality's sake. "What can we do to find out?"

"Watch him. That's the only thing you can do."

"You mean stake-out and tail him?" She couldn't believe she was saying that.

"Too many t-v shows. But yes, watch his house, see who comes and goes. Follow him when he leaves."

"What if I find something? What do I do?"

"Keep safe. Call the police."

After some further conversation Julia hung up and phoned Adam's house. Only an automated voice answered. She wished he'd get a cell phone, but he was an adamant holdout.

"Hi, it's me," she said into his recorder. "I'm going to be out tonight. I know you're doing something with the bog men, but I just wanted to let you know in case you were looking for me. You can get me on my cell if you need me."

She then called Martin to let him know about her conversation with McDermott. "No way," he said, "will I let you do a stake-out alone." He was coming right over.

Julia insisted on using her car rather than Martin's. His two-tone silvery taupe vehicle was too conspicuous, she argued. She had finally traded her old clunker in for a used black Toyota. Less noticeable. He relented.

They picked up coffee-to-go, which she hoped wouldn't send her looking for a bathroom before their vigil was over. It was almost eight o'clock. The moon would be nearly full but so covered by clouds, it couldn't be seen. They parked just down from Usha Kane's house, virtually, unbeknownst to her, where Adam had parked his car the preceding evening. There were no street lights anywhere in Sipponet and few homes had lamp posts, so they were enshrouded in darkness.

Before long, a large white pick-up drove towards them and turned into Usha Kane's driveway.

"Do you know who that is?" Julia asked.

Martin raised his head. "Ellis Chalmers. He has a big farm in Sipponet. He's a member of my congregation. As is Usha. I think they're friends."

"And brothers-in-law. His wife and Usha's wife are sisters."

"I didn't know that. But one thing I've learned over the years here is that there are so many relatives married to relatives, sometimes you think the whole county is related."

"Amen to that," she said under her breath.

"How did you learn that they were in-laws?"

Without revealing Esther's identity, she told him of a patient who believed the world is coming to an end because Usha Kane said so. "But I don't know whether he actually told her that or she imagined it. She's unreliable because of her mental illness. So I don't know how much to believe."

Julia leaned back against the seat and pushed her legs as far out as she could in front of her and stretched her back. She caught Martin looking at her out of the corner of his eye and she immediately collapsed her spine. She was glad it was too dark for him to see her blush. On the other hand, she reflected, he was the one who ought to blush. In fact, the more she thought about it, the more she—

"There's a car coming," Martin said. "Maybe we should duck."

They put down their heads simultaneously as the car passed them on the other side of the road.

"I hope the police don't patrol this area," Martin said, raising up. "It would be more than embarrassing to explain what we're doing here."

Or why I had my head down practically in his lap, she thought, but didn't dare say it. At least he didn't propose they pretend to be necking.

"There's another car," Julia said.

Lowering their heads, Martin said, "This is getting a little silly."

They waited for the car to pass and when it didn't, they both looked up towards Usha's house. The car, a pewter-colored sedan, was parked behind the pick-up.

"Do you know whose car that is?" Julia asked.

"No."

"Did you see him go in?"

"Nope. Maybe we can catch a glimpse on his way out."

After that, the road remained empty. Having spent a long day at work, Julia was more tired than she realized. She always seemed tired these days. Why was she so tired? She wasn't getting enough exercise, she decided. Just like Cat. She'd better start walking the dog every day instead of letting her out into the yard. And she'd better join a gym.

"They're leaving," she heard Martin say as she awoke with a start.

"Have I been asleep?"

"For a while."

"Sorry." She peered out the windshield. "Have they seen us?"

"I don't think so."

They both watched as first the car, then the truck pulled out of the driveway. It was nearly ten o'clock by Julia's watch.

At exactly 10:05, the livingroom lights in Usha Kane's house were turned out, followed by lights on upstairs, most likely the bedroom. At 10:30, the upstairs lights went out.

"What do you think?" Martin said.

"I don't think anything more is going to happen tonight, do you?"

"Probably not. Why don't we go home and get some sleep and start over again in the morning?"

"Agreed. I'll pick you up around six-thirty."

Martin made a face.

Julia smiled. "'Early to bed, early to rise.' We don't know what time he gets up. I'll bring sandwiches."

"Okay," he grimaced. "Six-thirty. I'll supply the coffee."

"I hope this isn't perfectly useless."

* * *

Usha Kane left his house at 11:30. They were all gathered to meet him in the far field.

"Is everything prepared for tomorrow night?" he greeted them as he inspected the area. The stone altar, the granite blocks in a semi-circle around the altar, were permanent and precise. What he was asking about was not the sacrificial site but the sacrifice.

Saturday, October 7ᵗʰ

At three a.m., the trucks began rolling onto The Cranberry Highway, one after another in a long unbroken convoy. With Adam and Cutter directing them, the logging trucks alternated with the cranberry trucks—with license plates reading Massachusetts and New Jersey.

By seven a.m., the news helicopters were circling the highway, reporting for the Boston and local television channels and police helicopters were radioing back to their base.

Adam and Cutter sat in Billy's livingroom over an early breakfast to watch the only television set among the three of them. None of them had slept that night. Adam had called Julia at home but there was no answer, so he left a message saying he'd catch up with her later.

"The sun rose this morning on a sea of undulating red," the Channel 5 News crew reported live from the lead helicopter. "The Cranberry Highway between Pittsley and Wareham is impassable at this hour. From up here, it looks like a corrugated patchwork of logs spaced every hundred feet across both lanes with cranberries lying in between. You cannot see the road for the red cranberries." The camera panned the highway in both directions. "The police estimate it will take hours, if not the entire day to clear the highway. The signs flanking what was the road read 'No Eminent Domain.'"

The camera zoomed in on a close up. Cutter made a pumping motion with his arm.

The newscaster narrated the closing shot. "Detours have been set up at either end of the highway and on the intersecting roads, but the police say the signs were not their doing. They don't know who put up the signs or who blocked the highway. We're not sure, at this hour, what this all means, but we will try to find out and report back to you as soon as possible. This is Darlene Nadjarian for Channel 5 News."

The camera switched back to the news studio where the male anchor was saying, "This just in. Our studio has received an anonymous message telling us that this highway protest is against the taking of residential land by eminent domain for the construction of a casino in the town of Pittsley, Massachusetts. We will attempt to reach town officials there for comment. Stay tuned."

"I sure would like to be a fly on the wall of Albert Carriou's house this morning," Billy said.

"He's going to be crazier than a shithouse rat," Cutter cackled.

* * *

The days were shortening. Pretty soon, sunrise would be at seven a.m. and sunset before six p.m. By the end of the month, daylight savings time would end and clocks all over the nation would be turned back. An hour would be gained in everyone's lives that had by consensus been banked for retrieval the previous April. Dawn would come earlier, a little after six, but now the sun would set before five p.m. October was a month of paradoxical transformation, Julia thought on her drive over to Martin's.

He was making coffee in the little kitchen when Julia arrived at six-thirty. She was accompanied by the housekeeper, Mrs. Whitcomb, just arriving for the day's work

Mrs. Whitcomb lived around the corner from the small church parish and had been the housekeeper there from the early days of the previous minister. She came once a week, always early on a Saturday morning so that she could be finished cleaning by Noon. The parish could ill afford a full-time housekeeper for their minister and Martin's self-sufficiency was a swaying advantage in being chosen Benjamin Chauncy's successor.

"Good morning, Reverend," she said cheerily as she entered the house. "You're starting early. I'll work in your office first, seeing as how you're busy in the kitchen."

"That'll be fine," Martin answered. "How do you take your coffee, Julia?"

"Milk, and however you like it."

He filled a large thermos with coffee, milk, and sugar.

"By the way," Mrs. Whitcomb said, "do you know you left yesterday's mail on the table in the foyer, Reverend? I'll put it on your desk, if you like."

"Never mind, Mrs. Whitcomb, I'll take it here. I forgot about it. Bills, I expect."

"I wouldn't mind forgetting about bills myself," she answered as she entered the kitchen. "But Mr. Whitcomb is one of those who's got to pay everything the day it comes in."

Martin smiled absently as she handed him a handful of envelopes.

"Mr. Whitcomb even pays the oil when we get the delivery slip. Doesn't even wait for a bill. I tell him not to be so eager to part with a dollar."

Martin's attention focused with a start on one particular envelope.

"I don't know why," she continued, "but Mr. Whitcomb can't stand to be in debt for anything. Not even a car. We never did have a credit card. 'If you can't pay for it, don't buy it,' he says."

As Martin flashed the envelope to Julia, she read the insignia of the Groton Congregational Evangelical Church, then checked at the date, Thursday October 5th. She looked at him in bewilderment.

"Mr. Whitcomb, he—"

"Excuse me, Mrs. Whitcomb, I don't mean to be impolite but I have to read this in my office right away. I'm finished now if you want to start in here. Julia?"

They left the housekeeper standing bewildered in the middle of the kitchen and went directly into his study and closed the door.

Throwing the other mail on the corner of the desk, he sat down and opened the portentous envelope with his marble-handled letter-opener. Even before reading the text, he looked for the signature.

"Benjamin." His eyes went up to the top of the page. "October 4th.

That was the night I talked with him. The night he...." He didn't complete the sentence.

"What does he say?"

Martin took a deep breath and read the letter.

My dear Martin,

When you called to ask me that terrible question—what did I know about the death of those innocents—I realized I could no longer hide from God's searching gaze.

Yes, I knew these men. I even believed in them, at first. I must have been in a delusion of demons for I understood them to be men of ultimate good intent.

How, you wonder, could I protect the sacrificers of little children? I wonder myself, and have no excuse other than that I did not know their evil deeds. They were my parishioners. I saw them every Sunday in church, every Tuesday at the men's Redemption Group, and at every beneficent function, for decades. I performed their marriage ceremonies, presided over the baptism of their children, brought them into communion.

Only later did I suspect the truth. But at the time, I never heard an accusation nor knew of any evidence against them.

I knew their beliefs about saving the world and appeasing God before his Final Destruction. I knew they had begun meeting outside the church. But I never believed their ideas were so extreme or that they would execute them. I looked away. I didn't want to know what they were doing.

But it preyed upon me. You know the other ways in which I attempted to relieve my guilt, to drown my conscience. I should have brought my suspicions to the police. But I didn't. In that, I am complicit in their crimes. My character is weak.

But when you told me of this latest child, the little boy, who was taken and is surely now dead, I knew I could not go on.

I point you in the direction of Usha Kane and Ellis Chalmers. Be stronger than I was, dear Martin, and follow where I could not.

Pray for me.

Benjamin

"Oh my God," she blurted.

Martin laid the pages on his blotter and his breaths came in short fast gulps. "Should we call Chief Burke?"

She paused and automatically passed her hand over her forehead and through her hair. "What can he do? There's still no real evidence, just suspicions. I think we should do what we planned. Go to Kane's house first. We can call Captain Burke as soon as we learn anything."

* * *

By the time Billy, Cutter, and Adam were finished with breakfast, with B.J. glued to the television, the announcer was saying, "We have not been able to reach the Pittsley Selectmen for comment, but we do have a representative for the townspeople affected by the move for eminent domain. Mr. Maxwell Kipper is a Boston attorney retained by the residents."

Adam and Cutter exchanged knowing looks.

"Turn it up, B.J., will you?" said Billy.

"Good morning, Mr. Kipper," came the voice over the television.

"Good morning."

"I understand that you represent the residents of Pittsley whose land is being proposed to be taken by eminent domain."

"That is correct."

"We'll get to the issue of this land being taken for the building of a casino and resort by a private developer. But first, I must ask you, Mr. Kipper, were you aware or involved in this incident of jamming up the highway with logs and cranberries?"

"I was neither involved nor aware of any such plans."

"That's why I had him leave the hall," Adam interjected.

"So this was carried out by the residents themselves?" the interviewer was saying.

"I have no knowledge of the participants."

Cutter laughed. "He said 'participants' not 'perpetrators.' I guess *we're* the perpetrators."

"And do you condone," probed the interviewer, "this unlawful act?"

"I don't condone any unlawful act."

Not getting anywhere with this line of questioning, the interviewer went on. "As you probably know, traffic has be interrupted all morning, inconveniencing a great many travelers on the road. The clean-up is going much more slowly than anticipated and it is now thought it will take the rest of the day to free the highway for vehicles again. These commuters are doubtless angry and frustrated about having to take sometimes-lengthy detours. Not to mention the cost of the clean-up. What do you think the protesters gained for all this negative reaction."

"I have no knowledge of what they expected to gain."

"Since you represent them—"

"I repeat, I represent the residents," Kip interrupted. "I am not a spokesman for the protesters."

"All right," the interviewer conceded, "then let's talk about the issue of eminent domain."

"Come to the floor of the Legislature on November sixth and you'll hear all about it."

"Is there anything else you can tell us?"

"No."

Frustrated, the newscaster wrapped it up and went on to the next story as the camera lingered on Maxwell Kipper looking very dignified.

"Well," said Cutter standing up. "Thanks mightily for breakfast, Billy. Now I'm going home, roger my wife, and sleep like a baby. Don't anybody call me before sundown."

"I should probably do the same," Adam said. "Except for the part about rogering your wife."

"What's that mean, 'roger'? B.J. asked.

"It's an old colonial term," Billy answered. "It means 'make love to.'"

"I'll have to use that sometime," B.J. grinned.

"Not until you're twenty-one," his father admonished.

"Or older, at the rate I'm going," B.J. said ruefully. He then turned his attention to Adam. "Are we going to look for the goats today, Adam?"

He was too tired to go anywhere today, but maybe today was the only chance he'd get. Tomorrow he had clinic hours in the morning and then the usual Sunday dinner with the crew. B.J. would have school on Monday.

"I guess we should. At least check it out." He shrugged. "I can sleep later. Just let me help your dad with the dishes."

"No need," Billy said, "I'll wash 'em fast and let them air dry. You go ahead with B.J."

"Okay, but we'll clear the table," Adam said as he began piling up the plates.

"Where are we going to start, Adam?" B.J. said enthusiastically as he got into the cab of Adam's truck.

"Let's go see what Dennis Buckley's up to. If he's like every other construction company, he'll be closing up at Noon on Saturdays."

"Why Mr. Buckley?"

Adam filled B.J. in on Joe Woods' van as they drove to the construction yard.

"Wow, you're like a real detective."

"Hardly."

"But Dad says you investigate animal cruelty cases and dog fights and cock fights and stuff."

"Sometimes."

B.J. sat back in the truck, satisfied that he'd made his point.

But Adam, in fact, had been doing fewer and fewer raids in his area. As bad as dogfighting and cockfighting had been before, it had changed for the worse over the past decade or more. It had moved into the cities with the waves of immigration and a different ethic had emerged. No longer were the bloodlines of the animals preserved, where champions had been bred to champions and pedigrees kept despite the illegal enterprise. No longer did the owners of the dogs or cocks conduct the fights by rules of the game, in an arena, with medical attention to the animals who survived. What the old guard saw was the taking over of the 'sport' by the city dwellers who had devolved it into a brutality even beyond the inherent brutality. Thus, the old country cock-fighters and dog-fighters had, for the most part, left the state for more congenial locations like upstate Maine, Louisiana, and West Virginia.

Poachers were in decline too. Not because of a change in attitudes but because of development. The open spaces were being sold off and new homeowners didn't want shotgun shells, rifle bullets, or arrows whizzing through the woods towards their children. Thus, Adam had less and less to investigate. The cruelty cases he saw now mostly were the obvious ones—neglect, abuse, ignorance. He hadn't raided a cockfight or tracked a poacher in years. Maybe that's why he was so intent on finding the stolen animals this time.

It was 11:15 a.m. when they reached Buckley Builders. The gate was already closed. There was no sign of activity and the silver BMW was gone. The sign on the chain-link fence read: "Monday-Friday, 8am-5pm; Saturday, 8am-11am; Sunday, closed."

"Damn. We just missed him," Adam muttered.

He pulled away from the street and drove to Buckley's home. There was no car and no sign of their quarry.

"Maybe he went to lunch," B.J. offered.

Adam cocked his head. "You know, that's a good idea." Buckley might indeed stop for lunch somewhere. "But where?" he pondered aloud.

"I bet he goes to Dottie's. That's where my friend's dad goes every Saturday. And he's in construction."

"No harm checking," Adam said. Buckley could have gone anywhere, but since he had no better idea, he decided to go with B.J.'s suggestion.

As they reached Dottie's, Adam was more than a little surprised to see Buckley's car parked in front.

"You were right, Beej. Good call."

The boy looked more than a little pleased and Adam was as glad as he was.

"You hungry?" he asked his companion.

"No, thanks. I ate a lot for breakfast."

"Me, too. Then we'll wait here until he comes out."

Adam settled back in his seat and B.J. did the same. Adam crossed his right ankle over his left knee and smiled to himself when he saw B.J. do likewise.

"How's things going in school, Beej?" he asked casually by way of passing the time.

"Pretty good, I guess."

"How are your grades?" Adam conjured up the image of B.J. leaning over his books yesterday.

"Mostly A's."

"You're in your...what...senior year?"

"I graduate next June."

"And then what, college?"

B.J. looked out the window, tilting his head away, and mumbled, "I don't know."

Adam frowned and looked closely at the boy. "Why not?"

B.J. just shrugged.

"Do you know what you want to do for a career?"

"Compose music," the boy said tentatively. "Classical music. And play the violin."

"Are you good at it?"

B.J. turned to look back at him with a shy smile. "I think so."

"Then you need to apply to Juilliard."

B.J. turned back to the window. "It's too expensive. And too far away."

Adam watched B.J. unconsciously spread his fingers on his thighs and dig in his nails. "Maybe you can get a scholarship."

"It would still be too far away."

"You can't be a father to your father, Beej. The last thing he'd want is for you to give up on your dreams for him. Your mother would tell you that if she were here."

"That's just it. She isn't."

"He'll get by without you. His friends will see to that. I'll see to that. You should apply to Juilliard and to Berklee College of Music in Boston. That's not so far. You could even try out for the BSO."

"The Boston Symphony Orchestra wouldn't possibly take me."

"How do you know?"

Adam went on to tell B.J. why he had to continue his education, and how he and his father's other friends would make sure everything was okay in the boy's absence. In the end, B.J. agreed to apply to at least four schools—the two Adam suggested plus the University of Massachusetts at Dartmouth and Boston University. They both agreed that he should probably apply to Pittsley Community College as a back-up; PCC served all of the region and had the lowest tuition.

"In the meantime," Adam counseled, "why don't you try out for the Plymouth Philharmonic and the New Bedford Symphony Orchestra? They're both close to home."

"I don't have my license yet," B.J. explained, "not until next month."

"If you need someone to go with you for your driver's test, I'll go," Adam offered. "We can practice over the next few weeks. Do you have a permit?"

B.J. nodded vigorously.

Adam opened the door of the cab and walked around to the passenger side. "Okay, slide over."

"Really?"

"Go."

B.J. slid behind the wheel, beaming.

"When Buckley comes out, you follow."

"Okay, Adam," B.J. answered eagerly.

It was nearly 1:30 p.m. before several men emerged from Dottie's.

"That's Jerry's dad." B.J. pointed out a huge man in jeans and a red-and-black lumberjacket.

Right behind them, Dennis Buckley came out and got into his car. B.J. started the truck and with Adam's instructions, followed him at a reasonable distance. Buckley pulled into the parking lot next to Dud's Suds. There was a line-up of pick-up trucks already in the lot. Adam told B.J. to park across the street and they watched as their quarry got out and walked into the bar.

"This may take a while, Beej. Do you need to go to the bathroom or anything?"

"Nope. I'm fine."

"There's a convenience store across the street if you want to grab something to eat or drink."

B.J. looked over. "Maybe a soda."

"Here, take this." Adam pulled out a twenty-dollar bill and handed it to B.J. "Why don't you get me a soda, too, and a couple of apples, bags of chips. They probably have some made-up sandwiches. Whatever you like."

"You don't think he'll come out before I get back?"

"Not a chance."

B.J. got out and went into the store. Adam made himself comfortable and watched the bar.

* * *

Parked where Julia and Martin could observe Usha Kane's house, she noticed that he had been very quiet for the past half-hour. She attributed it to Benjamin Chauncy's letter. She could almost feel his distress by the rigid way he was sitting and the pained expression on his face.

"I hope, Martin, that you're not still thinking you had anything to do with Reverend Chauncy's death."

Martin drew a deep breath. "I was thinking how bleak he must have felt. And why did he let it go on? No, what I really mean is why did God let it go on?"

He searched her face as though she would have an answer, but of course she didn't "What do you want me to say, Martin?"

"Nothing. I just don't understand how such cruelty and perversion emanate from a loving God."

"Then perhaps it doesn't," she said, more to mollify him than to engage in a theological exercise. But he wasn't about to let it go.

"I can only come up with two alternatives. Either there is no God—which is a thought I cannot accept—or the God I have devoted my life to is not the God I have always believed in."

"Then there must be another alternative." She was hoping he wouldn't continue on the subject. It was one she didn't feel very comfortable with herself.

"I'm trying to be logical about it." He began to speak, she thought, as if she weren't there. Or perhaps as if she shared his dilemma.

"If God exists, then He has to be indifferent to human suffering, or unable or unwilling to prevent it. Or perhaps suffering serves some higher purpose." He shook his head with his eyes cast forward. "But an indifferent, uncaring God is not worthy of worship. And if we humans deserve to suffer because of our corrupt natures, didn't Christ redeem us? That's the whole basis of my faith."

"Martin, you're not going to solve this one, and it's just causing you grief." But it was as if he didn't hear her.

"Nothing can convince me that Emily Chapman deserved her fate. Or any other abused child. Perhaps, in death, she will receive God's special blessing. But that begs the question. How can God avert His eyes to the wickedness? After all, what kind of beneficent God would allow such malice even for a higher purpose?"

Julia laid a consoling hand on his knee. "That question will just lead to more questions. Questions that Western theologians and philosophers have wrestled with for centuries. How could you presume to answer them and chastise yourself for failing?" She thought about Chaya Nim and Sam. "You know there are religions that evade the God-question altogether. Buddhism, for example. And some that aren't even monotheistic."

Whether it was her touch or her words, he turned to her. "Maybe that's the answer. Dualism. That there are two gods: the God who I proclaim every day and minute of my life; and a malevolent one of equal power. The other god, Satan."

"That wasn't exactly what I meant."

He looked out the window. "Yes, of course, that's blasphemy."

"Don't worry, I won't report you to the ecclesiastics," she said in jest. She was trying to draw him out of his despair and feeling wholly inadequate to the task. She could see he had come to a profound crisis in his faith, but this was not the time, this was not the place, and she was not the person with whom he should be having this conversation. She was a psychologist not a theologian. Despite her attempt to cajole him, he continued on.

"I have sometimes wondered if God and Satan have some mutual covenant about the course of human events...an agreement of non-interference. That, in granting free will to humankind to choose Evil, God allowed collateral damage. Like poor Emily. But is it because God does not win all the battles all the time? Or has He just forsaken us as an experiment gone bad?" Tears came to Martin's eyes and spilled down his cheeks. "Sorry," he said softly wiping them away.

"Martin, I don't know how to answer your questions. And I'm not sure anyone does."

"I think," he said candidly, "that I'm floundering." He took a deep breath. "I'm finding life's burden very heavy these days. And no one to share it with. Despite my busy workload ministering to the congregation, I'm lonely."

She knew that, not so long ago, he'd hoped that she might become someone who...but never mind, she'd just been angry with Adam at the time and...anyway, it wasn't to be. She was afraid he was going to say something to embarrass them both.

"I miss my wife," he said simply and leaned back against the headrest.

"Yes," she answered.

He closed his eyes. "Tell me, Julia, do you believe God has a purpose for us?"

"I don't know, Martin. The only thing I can do is try to find one for myself."

"Yes, perhaps it's all just a matter of choice."

He didn't amplify on that and Julia was not about to risk another foray into the labyrinthine subject. They remained silent until Julia looked at her watch.

"It's nearly two o'clock." They'd been there all morning and half the afternoon. "Your turn to catch a nap, Martin." Perhaps rest would take the edge off his emotions. "I'll wake you if he comes out."

But just then, Usha Kane's car began backing out of the driveway.

"I didn't see him come out," she said.

"He must have left by the back door."

She shivered. "This is it, then."

She had parked in the opposite direction from the route to Ellis Chalmer's house, hoping Usha wouldn't pass them on the way out. He didn't. He backed out of the driveway and took off in the direction they'd hoped he would.

* * *

It was a little after four o'clock when Dennis Buckley stepped out of Dud's Suds and drove off. B.J. and Adam followed.

"Where do you think he's going now, Adam?"

"I'm hoping he'll go to where the van is, so I can have a look at it."

"Why do you think Mr. Buckley stole the goats and calves?"

"Fall back just a little," Adam instructed. Then he answered, "We don't know that he did. But we may be able to prove that they were transported in a van that is in his custody. And if there's a reason to believe there're been animals in the van, I can charge him pending investigation."

"You can?"

"Oh yes."

Although he had powers of arrest from the State Police, it had been a while since Adam had exercised them for anything but animal cruelty cases. But this was still within his mandate.

As they followed, Buckley turned onto the road leading to Ellis Chalmers' farm.

"Interesting," Adam said under his breath.

B.J. glanced at him inquiringly, so he explained about Joe Woods and the Chalmers as they dropped back a little.

As they neared the entrance to the farm, Adam saw a car parked down the road and off to the side that looked suspiciously familiar. Buckley turned into the farm and he signaled B.J. to drive past the entrance, as far as the car beyond. As they came close, he identified the black Toyota.

"That's Julia's car." But there was no one in it. What was Julia doing here?

B.J. parked the truck behind her car and handed Adam the keys as they got out.

"We'll cut through the woods and come out on the other side. That way we can get a look around back," Adam said.

As they trekked through the underbrush, Adam felt a strange sense of foreboding. What if they were discovered and B.J. was with him?

They broke into the clearing in the back of the field. It was pastureland that must once have had cows grazing there before the collapse of the dairy industry in the state. It had been kept a pasture for the haying. There appeared to be at least twenty acres of open field.

"Adam, look!" B.J. whispered, pointing.

At the far end of the field was a pen with one goat, a Saanen billygoat.

"Is that him?" Billy asked.

"Shh," Adam said. "Go back to the truck."

"What?"

"Go back to the truck."

"What are you going to do?"

"Never mind. Go back to the truck. Now."

"But—"

"Now, B.J."

B.J. reluctantly turned around and began walking back through the woods. Thankfully, Adam told himself, the boy hadn't seen the stone pit on the other side of the field near the house. It was likely that the other animals had already been slaughtered and cooked. So Goody was wrong, they *had* been for barbecue. But whoever is eating these animals, Adam mused, has a gourmet taste for very expensive meat.

He skirted around the field, hugging the wooded perimeter. The sun was low in the west; it would set in half an hour. The sky was already turning vibrant with colors of pink and orange. This side of the field was already in shadow.

Ordinarily, he would just go to the door, barge in when it was opened and arrest Ellis Chalmers. But he had to be more wary, what if Julia were in there? But why? If she were going to pick up some squash or turnips or whatever, why wouldn't she have driven to the Chalmers' farmstand down the street? To the best of his knowledge, she had never met the Chalmers. He would have to go in, but go in cautiously.

As he was about to walk up the farmhouse, he spotted Usha Kane's car parked in back. He didn't like the idea that Usha might be in there with Julia after what his son had tried to do.

As he paused, another car drove in. Followed by another pick-up truck. And another. He stood watching as four more pick-ups pulled in. He tried to see the occupants as they got out, but they were turned away from him. They seemed to greet each other wordlessly and enter not by the front door but by the rear basement door. Then Dennis Buckley drove in with his unmistakable BMW. Was this the Parkwood Development Corporation? They had to be scrambling after this morning's very public protest.

Obviously, he had stumbled on some sort of meeting. But what did Julia have to do with it? And why had she parked where she parked? The only conclusion he could come to was that she was visiting Evie Chalmers for some reason. But wouldn't she have driven up to the front of the house if that were the case?

Maybe, he told himself, she ran out of gas. Or had car trouble and pulled over the side of the road and walked up to the house to use the phone. But no, she had her cell. She could have called him. Except, of course, he hadn't been home since last night.

He proceeded towards the farmhouse and around to the front. The inside door was open behind the screened door. He rang the bell. It seemed to take an inordinate amount of time for Evie Chalmers to get there.

She peered through the screen at him. "Oh, it's Adam, isn't it?"

"Yes. I was driving by and I saw my…fiancées'…car on the side of the road. Julia Arnault? Is she here?"

"Why, no. I'm afraid I don't know her. She's not here."

He stood with his hands in his pockets, looking steadily at her. "I thought maybe her car broke down."

"I'm afraid I don't know anything about it. I'm sorry I can't help you." She began to close the inside door.

"Perhaps your husband might know?" he persisted.

"I'm sure not. He's been very busy."

"Do you think I might ask him?" This felt wrong.

"I'm sorry. He's very busy right now."

"Perhaps I could use your telephone?"

She hesitated, then said, "You'll have to forgive me for not inviting you in. I don't let anyone in if I don't know them well. But if you give me her number, I'll call it for you."

Adam gave her the number and she disappeared inside. As he looked up into the darkening sky, he could see the full moon still faint in the twilight.

After a few minutes, Evie returned.

"I dialed it and let it ring for quite a while, but there was no answer. So I dialed it again and got a message that the phone number is out of range. I'm sorry but I have to get back to my cooking."

"Could you do me one more favor then? Could you please call the Pittsley Police Station and ask Captain Burke to meet me here?"

She hesitated again.

"Is it a police matter?" she finally asked.

"Yes. It may be."

"I see. Well, um, just give me a couple of minutes then."

When she came back, she unlocked the screen door.

"Captain Burke said he'll be over shortly. Why don't you come in and have a cup of tea. I was just making some for myself."

The screen door slammed behind him as he followed her into the kitchen.

She placed two cups of tea on the table, saying, "It's jasmine," and asked if he took milk. He did.

"I have some chocolate éclair pie, would you like a piece?"

"No thank you, the tea is fine." It actually wasn't so fine. It tasted like perfume. Nobody, he concluded, serves plain anything anymore. Even coffee has at least half-a-dozen flavors. None of which he liked. "What kind of meeting is your husband having?"

"Meeting?" Evie had her back to him, stirring the cast-iron pot with a wooden spoon.

"I saw all the vehicles parked in back."

"Oh. That's his fishing club. They sit around and tell tall tales and plan their next camping trip. Do you fish?"

"Not vreally." Did he just slur his words?

"Ellis loves fishing. I think it's just to get away from me sometimes. Are you married, Adam? Of, course not," she corrected herself, "you're engaged. To the woman you were looking for."

He was feeling lightheaded. Then he thought of B.J. in the truck. He should let him know where he is.

Adam started to get up and began to sway. He held onto the table for support.

"Are-you-all-right?" Her words sounded low and slow, as if it were a record winding down.

Adam tried to answer but his tongue simply wouldn't fit into his mouth. The table tipped and the cup and saucer went flying. He sank down into his chair but couldn't seem to stay there. He slid onto the floor, the chair backing out from under him. He tried to get up but his legs wouldn't work. He could still see and hear but it all seemed to be far away.

He saw two pair of workboots next to his head. Was his head on the floor? Looking up, he saw the grey-bearded face of Usha Kane going through his pockets. He removed a set of keys.

"Go downstairs," he instructed Evie, "and tell Donald and Simon to take his truck and her car and pull them around back. I told them to do that first thing, but they didn't. Now we've got this one."

"What'll you do with him, Usha?" asked Evie Chalmers.

"We'll worry about that later."

"But that makes three of them."

"I said we'll worry about it later. Go get Donald and Simon."

Three? He could only think about Julia. They had Julia. And who else? Evie had said 'three.' Did they have B.J.? But he couldn't seem to concentrate.

"Give me a hand, Ellis," Usha was saying to an older man Adam did not know. But Dennis Buckley was standing behind him. "Dennis, you take his feet. We'll put him in the pantry for the time being."

They pulled rather than lifted him along the floor.

Then everything went black.

Whatever drug Evie Chalmers had put in his tea was beginning to wear off. Probably because he didn't drink all of it. But he was still woozy. He looked around, taking inventory of his situation. He was able to make out that the pantry was a square room with two sides lined with floor-to-ceiling built-in shelves.

Then Adam heard what sounded like a scream. His first thought was of Julia and he immediately tried to get up. His initial attempt was unsuccessful. His legs wouldn't support him and he slid back on his rump and tried to gather strength.

How long had he been out? Not long, he thought, but there was no way of telling. Out of the small window at the back of the pantry, it was nearly dark. He had to get out of here. Julia may have been harmed and here he was, completely helpless.

By sheer will, he gradually pulled himself up onto his feet, grabbing onto the sturdy shelves. There was an overhead lightbulb with a string hanging down. He switched it on and in the bright glare he saw the shelves were completely full with Mason jars of preserved fruit and vegetables.

He tried the doorknob and found it locked. They might have left the key in the doorlock. But that wouldn't be much help. He'd have to poke it out onto a paper and pull the paper back under the door with the key on it. There was no way any key was going to fit under that door. He wasn't even sure a piece of paper would fit under it.

What were his choices? He could try to break down the door. Good luck there. He'd probably blow-out his shoulder before the door would budge. Plus they'd certainly hear it.

But the window was too small for him to get through.

His thoughts were riveted on Julia. What have they done with her? Why was she there in the first place? This couldn't be just about the missing animals. She was more interested in—suddenly it all clicked. Julia was interested in Ponlok. This must have something to do with Ponlok Nim.

He could only hope that B.J. was safe in the truck. He wished he had left the keys. Had he put the boy in danger?

He was aware that his thoughts were still disorganized. As he leaned against the shelving furiously trying to think of a way out, the doorknob turned, then stopped. He grabbed the nearest weapon, a Mason jar filled with sliced peaches, ready to assault whoever opened the door and make his escape. Some weapon, he thought to himself.

The key turned in the lock and the door opened. Adam was about to swing the thick glass jar into the face of the man on the other side of the door when he caught himself.

"Beej!" he whispered hoarsely.

"Adam," said the boy equally whispering, "I thought they might have killed you."

"Not yet. What are you doing here?"

"I was waiting in the truck for about twenty minutes when I had to pee. I got out of the cab and walked about fifteen feet into the woods. After I finished I heard voices on the road, so I watched from the woods. Two men were there, and one of them got into your truck and started it up."

"Who were they?"

"I don't know. But I knew you didn't leave your keys in the truck and there wasn't enough time for the man to cross the wires. Meanwhile, the second man unlocked the driver's side door to Julia's car and got in. So I figured you must be in trouble. And there aren't any other houses around to get a phone, so I came in."

"Nobody saw you?"

"No, they're all outside in the field. There's a bonfire, and some kind of altar."

"Altar?" Was that what he thought was a barbecue pit?

"They're all wearing white cloaks. About ten or eleven of them. And they've killed the goat. He screamed when them lifted him onto the altar. Then they chanted. Then they slit his throat with some big knife. That's when I ran into the house while they were all busy."

That was the scream he must have heard, Adam realized with a degree of relief.

"It was really weird," B.J. continued. "Did you find Miss Julia?"

"No. But she's got to be here somewhere."

"I looked everywhere when I was looking for you. There's nobody upstairs in the bedrooms and nobody else down here."

"Did you go in the tractor barn?"

"No. Just the house."

"I'll look there. You stay here and call the police."

"I already did. As soon as I got in the house, I called Captain Burke."

"Good show, Beej. You get out to the road and hide until you see the police cars. I've got to find Julia."

"But I want to stay with you, Adam."

"No. Do what I say. I can move faster alone."

"Didn't do so good before," B.J. mumbled.

Adam took the boy by the shoulders. "You're right. I'd still be locked in there without your help. But I don't want to worry about keeping you safe while I'm looking for Julia. Understand?"

"Yes," B.J. said grudgingly.

They left the house by the back door, staying close to the foundation. Adam could see the bonfire with the full moon nearly over it. Just as B.J. had said, there were cloaked figures around the fire and they were chanting. One tall figure hovered over the body of the goat. They looked, he thought fleetingly, like Druids. The tall cloaked figured looked up toward the sky and in the moonlight, Adam recognized him as Usha Kane. He was torn between running over there and...and doing what, exactly? He was unarmed. And these men would most likely not be unarmed.

He sent B.J. around to the front of the house with instructions to keep to the edge of the driveway near the trees and he ran across from the house to the tractor barn. Adam carefully slid open one half of the barn doors part-way. It was dank and cavernous inside.

The floor of the barn was packed earth. He could make out a tractor and a bulldozer side-by-side, along with a hayrake attachment, a rototiller, a lawnmower tractor, farm equipment against the walls. At the same time he heard a muffled voice and he spotted a huddled figure in the corner on the ground: Julia, bound and gagged. And beside her, Martin Ryman.

Adam didn't even take time to think, but went immediately to her. He pulled the duct tape off her mouth.

"Oh, Adam, thank God."

"Are you all right?"

"Yes. I think she drugged us."

As he looked around for something to cut the ropes, B.J. suddenly appeared behind him and handed him a Swiss Army Knife.

"You're not supposed to be here. We'll talk about this later." Adam took the knife and cut Julia's wrists and ankles free. Then he did the same for Martin. He wanted to ask why Martin was with her, but this was not the time.

"The police are coming," Adam said to Julia. "All we have to do is wait here."

"No," said Julia. "They've got Ponlok. They're going to sacrifice him."

"Sacrifice?"

"I'll explain later. While you're scolding B.J.," she reprimanded.

"At the same time you can tell me what he's doing here." Adam glared at Martin. While he didn't exactly consider him a rival, not anymore, he wasn't pleased to see that Julia had had him accompany her. But no time now. He'd find out later.

"Where's Ponlok?" B.J. asked.

"We don't know," Martin said. "He's not in here."

"And he's not in the house," said Adam.

"He might be," B.J. said. "I wasn't looking for him, I was looking for you. So I started upstairs and found you downstairs. I didn't go into the basement."

"There's another door from the outside. I saw them go in that way," Adam said.

"Then we should look there," Martin said, "before they bring him out."

Adam went to the door, with Martin close behind. He was about to make a run for the basement door when he abruptly pulled back, nearly knocking Martin down.

"What's the matter?"

Adam held up his hand. "They're bringing him out of the basement," he whispered.

"He's dead!" B.J. said.

"No, he's twitching," Adam replied. "He's probably drugged."

"We've got to do something," Julia demanded, "before it's too late."

"And we can't wait for the police," Martin added.

"Don't you have a gun, Adam?" B.J. asked.

"No."

"I'm going out to talk to them," Martin said. "They're my parishioners."

"What are you, nuts?" Adam grabbed his arm.

"I know these men. I'm their minister." Martin shook his arm free.

"Which is why they hog-tied you in here and were planning to kill you."

"They wouldn't have done that."

"The hell they wouldn't. They're about to murder a little boy. They've killed other little children for years. What makes you think they'd stop at you?"

Martin turned away from him and addressed Julia. "I don't think that's their intent. They could have already killed me. And you. And him. That's not what this is about."

"Maybe not us," she said, "but they are going to kill Ponlok."

"No they aren't." Martin suddenly catapulted past Adam, who tried to make a grab for him.

"Shit!" Adam punched the wall with his fist. "Julia, stay here with B.J. until the police come. I'm going to go get him." He crouched around the barn door and was gone.

* * *

"I bet there are guns in the house," B.J. said to Julia as she peered out into the darkness. "Probably in the basement. That's where my friend Jerry's dad keeps his."

It would probably be safer in there anyway, she thought. They already knew she was in the tractor barn and they just might come looking for her there and find B.J., too.

"Okay, let's make a run for it. While they're distracted. On three."

B.J. nodded. Julia counted to three and they dashed out. A shot rang out just as they got to the door. B.J. turned quickly to check on Julia, who was just seconds behind him.

She froze when she heard the gunshot. 'God, please don't let that have been Adam,' she prayed. B.J. ran back, yanked her hand and pulled her into the doorway.

"I'm all right," she said breathlessly, "go in." She followed and closed the door and locked it.

When B.J. flicked on the light switch, he gasped. The room looked like a chapel.

There were three rooms off to the left. One of the doors was open, the other two were closed.

"Check behind the other doors," Julia said, as she went to the first room. From the light in the chapel, she could see in. It looked like a prison cell. 'This must be where they kept him,' she thought.

"This is just a big closet," B.J. said as he opened the farthest door. "Looks like all kinds of church stuff."

They both moved on to the middle door. Julia turned the knob but the door was locked.

"Look for a key," she said to B.J.

"You look for a key, I'll try to jimmy it," B.J. said, taking out his knife and choosing a small blade.

Julia prowled the room, feeling over the doorjambs, looking under altar cloths, candelabras, bowls.

"Got it!" shouted B.J.

Julia turned around as he opened the door. Inside the room were racks of rifles of all sorts, along with handguns and what looked like grenades.

"Good Lord." Julia lifted down one of the rifles. "Do you know anything about these things?" she asked B.J.

"Not really. I think you just point and shoot."

"But is it loaded?"

"I bet it is."

She slung the rifle belt over her shoulder and grabbed another one. "Put one on and stay here. I'll get one to Adam." *He has to be there*, she told herself.

* * *

In the light from the bonfire, Adam watched as Martin held up his hands and approached Usha Kane and the other cloaked men.

"Stop this, Usha! You have to stop this. You don't know what you're doing!"

One of the men shot at Martin's feet and the minister halted. Adam debated rushing them but he knew they'd probably begin shooting at both of them, and not just at their feet. He'd have to circle around and take one of the men down and get his rifle. He'd seen Julia and B.J. cross over to the house basement; at least they were safe for now.

"Stay right where you are, Reverend," he heard Usha say. "We don't want to hurt you but we will if we have to."

"But why? Why are you doing this?"

"It has to be done, and done tonight." Usha looked up at the sky. "For all our sakes."

In his robe, his eyes dark in his gaunt face, he looked like a picture of the martyrs Adam had seen in his catechism so many years ago. There was a fervor about him that made him seem imposing, almost invincible. It was hard to imagine Usha Kane as the once-mayor of a little country village.

"Explain it to me, Usha." Martin moved closer. "Explain this horror you're about to commit."

"It gives us no pleasure to sacrifice this child," Usha replied. "We are not crazy, Reverend. And we're not evil. Or Satanic, or bloodthirsty. We are only doing what we have to."

"No. That's not true."

"Go back to your Bible, Pastor. God has always demanded sacrifices."

"Not live sacrifices. Not anymore." Martin moved a little closer to the altar.

Usha threw out his arms. "When we stopped sacrificing is when the world began to feel His wrath. You can't deny we've come to the brink of extinguishing ourselves."

"But if that's true, it's our fault, not God's vengeance."

Usha lowered his arms. "Our impending doom is a consequence of God's displeasure. We are sinners in the hands of an angry God."

All Adam could think of was the fire-and-brimstone colonial preachers that followed after the Puritans. To them, every disaster, natural or manmade, was retribution for a their wicked ways. These men—and he gradually realized that there was one woman among them, Evie Chalmers—these people were throwbacks.

"Jonathan Edwards," Martin replied. "His sermon in Enfield, Connecticut, 1741."

Yes, thought Adam, I remember that. Jonathan Edwards and The Great Awakening. But that was as much as he could recall.

"And he said," Usha continued, *The wrath of God burns against them, their damnation does not slumber; the pit is prepared, the fire is made ready, the furnace is now hot, ready to receive them; the flames do now rage and glow. The glittering sword is whet, and held over them, and the pit hath opened its mouth under them. The devil stands ready to fall upon them, and seize them as his own, at what moment God shall permit him. They belong to him; he has their souls in his possession, and under his dominion.*

"Thus far, we have assuaged God with our sacrifices. And He has stayed His hand from our total annihilation. But things have gone too far now and unless He is honored and appeased, we are all doomed."

Martin edged closer. "You're wrong. God cannot be appeased. He only requires our—"

"—worship," finished Usha.

"Yes. But not this sort of worship."

"Who are you to say?"

Ignoring that, Martin said, "You killed and mutilated and raped all those other children, all those little girls. You think that's worship?"

Usha stepped forward towards the altar, perpendicular to Martin at his right shoulder, and Adam could see his long face in profile.

"We didn't do that. Their deaths were swift and painless. They were never conscious. The transgressions happened after the sacrifice. By Floyd Mather and Babe Hampley. If we had known what they were doing, we would have stopped it. All we did was take the hearts. No different from practices throughout time."

"Evil practices," said Martin.

"There is no more time for this."

"But we're witnesses," Martin said. "We can testify against you? What are you going to do with us?"

The others had gathered in a circle around the altar.

"You didn't tell me why it had to be tonight," Martin persisted. "Why tonight?"

Usha bowed his head, then approached Ponlok, lying unconscious on the altar. He raised the ceremonial knife.

There was no time for Adam to execute his plan. "Stop!" he shouted, hoping to draw away their attention.

But in that instant, Martin dashed forward and hurled himself between the man and the boy, impaling himself onto the knife.

Time seemed to stop for Adam. He never heard the basement door open until Julia came running to him with a rifle.

Snapping into action, he quickly took the rifle from her. It was an M1-Garand, not the newest model but one he was familiar with. He expertly checked it, determined it was loaded, and in one motion aimed it at Usha Kane, squeezing off a single shot.

The man's head exploded and he fell backward onto the ground a foot away from Martin's body. He couldn't tell whether or not Martin was dead, but he wasn't moving.

"Get back inside!" he yelled to Julia.

Two of the men bent over Usha while one of them, who Adam recognized as Dennis Buckley, said something to the others. Adam pushed Julia back towards the basement and flattened himself against the wall.

They don't know who shot Usha yet, he thought. *They probably think I'm still in the house, and Julia is in the tractor barn. I'd better make my move now.*

* * *

As Julia reached the open basement door, she saw B.J. raise his rifle and point it somewhere beyond Adam's right shoulder.

There were two shots in succession as she slid into the doorway. Adam followed, pulling both her and B.J. in with him.

"I think I hit him." B.J. said to Adam. "He was going to shoot you."

"Where's Martin?" Julia asked frantically.

"He's been stabbed."

Julia clutched his arm. "Is he alive?"

"I don't know."

"Adam—"

"Give me the other rifle, Julia. You two stay in here. Lock the door after me."

"You can't go out there," she protested.

But in an instant he'd grabbed the second rifle, slung it over his shoulder, and was gone again.

B.J. closed and locked the door as Julia stood with a stricken look on her face.

"He'll be all right," B.J. said confidently, "Adam was a sniper in Vietnam."

"Yes," Julia replied. What she didn't say was that after the war, Adam never wanted to use a weapon again. He never carried one, even though he had a license. He hated killing. Because, he had told her one night, he was so very good at it.

* * *

As soon as he'd closed the door, Adam immediately dropped to the ground with his rifle ready. The man B.J. shot was on his back and holding his groin. Dennis Buckley was nowhere to be seen, but another man was approaching Martin's prone body. If Martin's not dead now, Adam thought, he soon will be.

But the man passed by Martin and brandished a machete-sized knife over the altar where Ponlok lay, obviously to conclude what Usha had started. Adam aimed for his shoulder and fired. The man yelped and spun around, the machete flying out of his hand. He grabbed his shoulder and dropped to his knees. Adam put another shot into his other shoulder. The man fell to the ground on his face.

He could hear police sirens in the distance. It wouldn't be long before they were here. His quick glance took in the boy, Ponlok, lying on the stone altar and the remaining cloaked figures, including Evie Chalmers, running towards the house. Except Dennis Buckley. He would worry about the others later. Right now, he had to find Buckley. Where did he go?

His eyes scanned the landscape of possibilities. Wherever Buckley was, he hadn't run into the house with the others. And he wasn't shooting at Adam.

Then he saw the silver BMW pulling away from the other parked vehicles.

Of course, Adam realized, he'd go for his car.

Adam swiftly got up and ran to the closest vehicle, his own pick-up truck that someone had driven there. There was little likelihood, even if the key was in the ignition, that he could catch up with Buckley. He was just going to have to take the long shot.

He rested the rifle on the hood of the truck, aimed at Buckley's rear tire as he drove away and pulled the trigger. The tire went flat and the car swerved. Adam aimed again and hit the second rear tire, then the gas tank.

Now at a complete stop, Dennis Buckley jumped out of his car, shedding his cloak as he ran for the woods. Adam took aim again. Got Buckley in the ass. And probably through the hip and whatever else. He went down just as two cruisers came racing up the driveway.

Adam ran over to Ponlok. The boy was breathing, but unconscious.

Martin was dead.

Sunday, October 8th

There was a cold wind, unrelenting rain, then a frost overnight that wilted the leaves of any remaining vegetable plants left in the backyard gardens, and left a thin crystal coating of ice on the back decks and the hoods of cars left out of garages. The bog owners had flooded the bogs to protect the vines and farmers had covered their pumpkins until the sun came up.

Exhausted both physically and emotionally, Julia and Adam slept late, bundled in the warm comforter on Adam's bed against the raw chill of the morning. They lay entwined as though holding each other safe from the horror of the night before.

"Do we have to get up?" Julia asked, mindful that this was Sunday and she couldn't recall a single Sunday since she'd known Adam that he'd skipped his dinner ritual with his friends.

"Not today."

He pulled her tighter to him and she closed her eyes again trying not to think of anything except his embrace, the feel of his skin against hers, their rhythmic breathing together. And thus they both fell back to sleep.

Ultimately, they could no longer avoid the day. Yes, there was relief in the rescue of Ponlok and the arrest of Usha Kane's followers. But they would have to see to Martin's funeral. Did he have any family left to notify? Did he leave instructions for his funeral or burial? He would probably want to be with his wife and children. They would have to find out if he had a will, named an executor. All the things that no one seemed to know. He had been more solitary than anyone had imagined.

They had showered, dressed, and gone downstairs in virtual silence, each preoccupied with thoughts of what had happened the previous night. Over coffee—neither of them had wanted breakfast—Adam finally said, "He was pretty courageous to do what he did. Stupid maybe, but courageous."

"More than that," she answered. "When we were parked out in front of Ellis Chalmer's house last evening, Martin told me he was experiencing doubts about his faith. And yet, when he faced death, he acted without hesitation."

"Of course, he didn't know we had an arsenal of rifles."

She gave him a chiding look.

"But," he added hastily, "he probably would have done the same thing anyway to save Ponlok. The fact is, I do think he was courageous. It was easy for me to shoot from a sniper's distance. He walked right up to them, come what may."

"Maybe for him, there was no other choice." She reflected for a moment, then asked, "Do you believe in Heaven, Adam?"

He grimaced. "Haven't thought much about it since I was thirteen or so."

"Neither have I. But he missed his wife so much, wouldn't it be nice if there were one? I'd like to believe there is, for his sake."

He looked up with a hardness in his eyes. "They believed in Heaven, those people. They believed in Hell. And the Apocalypse. And look what came of it."

"But anything can be perverted. Even good intentions."

"Especially good intentions."

She looked out his back window over the garden that had already been culled, where the last of the tomato plants had wilted to the ground like someone in a dead faint. The wind and rain had stripped most of the trees of their leaves and they covered the ground, already turning brown in the daylight. Only the yellow beach leaves remained like a sunlit beacon in the woods.

"The leaves are off the trees," she said, stating the obvious. "We're coming into winter early." Then she turned back to him. "I worked it out with Sam yesterday to change my status to part-time at the hospital. As of January 1st."

"Oh?"

He sounded apprehensive, she thought. "And I had a long talk with Lt. McDermott and he was able to link me up with Captain Morrow of the State Police. They have some funding for a forensic psychologist. It's not much money but I can swing it with my part-time salary at the hospital. It'll be on a trial basis, of course, for the start. But who knows? Maybe this is what I should be doing." She paused. "What do you think?"

Adam took a deep breath. "I know you don't need my approval, but maybe it's something you have to do. You won't know unless you try. There is one thing, though."

"Which is?" She raised her eyebrow at him.

"You know each time you've gotten involved in these investigations, you had back-up."

"Meaning you?"

"Meaning me."

"What are you implying?" She knew her tone was defensive. Was he suggesting she wasn't capable of doing this on her own?

"Give me a minute."

He disappeared upstairs and returned just as quickly. While she was wondering why he was being so cryptic, Adam reached into his pocket and withdrew a black velvet ring box.

"It was my mother's."

Julia took the box delicately, almost holding her breath.

"It's not a very big diamond, but I'm hoping it will do."

As she opened it, her expression became soft and her eyes filled up. "It will do very well."

He took the box and removed the one-karat diamond solitaire set in white gold. "I can have it made smaller if it doesn't fit."

But the ring slipped on her finger perfectly.

"Don't think this is like an actual engagement, you know," he said. "It's nothing definite."

"I know," she said smiling.
"Not marriage. Not yet anyway."
"I know."
Then he leaned over and kissed her.

Monday, November 6th

Adam sat in the gallery of the State House in Boston, along with Julia, Amos Hall, Billy, and B.J. as Maxwell Kipper, Attorney-at-Law, took the floor in favor of a bill introduced by a state representative from Springfield. No Boston politician would sponsor the bill and one-by-one Kip and Adam had gone down the list until they found one, just one, who agreed to do it. She said modestly that she was a distant descendent of Daniel Shays and held the principles of the Rebellion dear to her heart, this old white-haired woman who had been a real estate lawyer. "Land squabbles," she'd told them, "are my meat and potatoes." But the State taking private property willy-nilly, "No, never. Not over Daniel's dead body or mine."

Kip introduced himself to the body politic and illustrated the reasons for this particular bill, including the controversy in Pittsley.

"Fortunately, circumstances prevailed," he told them, "and the town rescinded its plan."

The members of the Legislature who knew about the Cranberry Highway Revolt smiled behind their hands. But they were not aware, Adam knew, of the entire story—that several members of a sacrificial cult charged with the abduction and attempted murder of Ponlok Nim (albeit with insufficient evidence of the other murders) were officers of the Parkwood Development Corporation that originally instigated the eminent domain grab. Unfortunately, at least in Adam's mind, they did not include Conny Cranshaw. If he had been present, and Adam couldn't be certain one way or the other, he'd gotten away.

"Property ownership," Kip began, "is a relatively recent concept. That is," he smiled unctuously, "since the dawn of human civilization. And of course, territoriality precedes even that. You might say it's genetic. But before the idea that pieces of the earth could be bought and sold, there was the practice of 'Userfrucht' meaning 'if you use it, it's yours to use.' And much of that had to do with who got there first." He paused for effect and looked around. Seasonally, Native Americans, for the most part, followed the food, sometimes migratory food, sometimes stationery food—and by that I include, for example, grains, maize, and…cranberries."

Kip now began to pace a little back and forth, matching his words to his stride. "But to produce an actual piece of paper, a title, to land that was held in common, proclaiming ownership, well that was introduced only a few centuries ago. Imagine it. Right here in Massachusetts, a 'land grant' was given to the colonists from English shareholders to land they did not even own." Kip raised his hand in a theatrical gesture of disbelief.

"However," now his voice became strident, "for four hundred years, we have lived here with the premise that if you own the land—by buying it, inheriting it, or acquiring it through gift or debt—it is your property."

He glanced up at Adam, who silently acknowledged that Kip was following the script. The object, Adam thought, as he looked down at the members seated in the hall, was to inform them, guide them, then slam-dunk them without losing their interest. So far, so good.

"We understand," Kip continued, "that the right of ownership is not absolute. The State and Federal governments exercise some uniform liens on individual properties. They can seize land for nonpayment of taxes and keep it or auction it off to the highest bidder. They regulate what you may store on your property; what you may build on it; what you may do or not do if it interferes with your neighbor, violates town ordinances, is illegal or threatening to public health and safety. And the list goes on."

Kip had deliberately chosen to use the pronoun 'they' rather than 'you' to the legislators so as to distance them from the abstract government and put them on the side of the citizens. As Adam scrutinized their faces, it seemed to be working.

Kip turned and looked directly at the House Speaker. "So what does it really mean to say you own your land when, in fact, what we really do is lease our property under specific conditions. Government agrees to allow us to keep and use our land within these conditions. In turn, this contract has always meant that neither the Federal, State, nor Municipal governments would act arbitrarily or proceed in self-interest against its residents. Only in extreme conditions would the government compel us to forfeit our Userfrucht property. One of the compelling reasons is public betterment, such as highways, schools, hospitals and the like. What is not an extreme circumstance is a casino. What is not an extreme circumstance is town's elected officials determining that they can obtain more revenue from a corporation than a resident or group of residents, and that this financial gain supersedes out land rights." Kip lowered his voice to an ominous tone and turned back to the audience. "Once you have done that, honorable Members of the House, you put us all in jeopardy. We are at the mercy of the authorities in power. How do we ensure that that power is exercised justly? Only by limiting it."

Adam saw scattered heads bobbing. But was it enough?

Kip held up a piece of paper. "This bill will limit the taking of land by eminent domain to clearly specified, legitimate instances of public benefit. It further requires that any effort to take land for reasons other than on this list must be put to statewide plebiscite, a vote of the common people. Only domestic emergencies are exempted from referendum and those must be signed by the Governor and ratified by the Legislature. No law is perfect or will cover all conditions. But the principle is important to uphold as Our Founders intended it. We are, after all, not the State but the *Commonwealth* of Massachusetts. We are not Connecticut."

On the affirmative vote in favor of the bill, the Town of Pittsley not only abandoned all plans for the casino, it declined to prosecute the perpetrators of the Cranberry Highway Revolt or to reveal their names, the ones they suspected at least, to the authorities.

The 'parties' all assembled at the American Legion that evening for a celebration. Amos Hall shook Elgin Bradburn's hand, neither of them speaking but both nodding at each other like fighters who have fought a good fight and are returning to their respective corners.

Elgin was seen later cornering Fiona Hathaway in conversation and that indomitable woman was smiling like a schoolgirl.

Cutter, his wife Angel, Billy, Adam, and Julia sat at a corner table along with B.J. and his friend, Lucky. Lucky was able to convince his mother to let him celebrate his rescue with his friend. Only Tully and Goody were missing. Tully said he had work to do and he'd never intended to let anyone take his land anyway, so what was all the fuss about? As for Goody, he didn't hold with partying and drinking. Last party he went to, he said, was Cutter's wedding. Wouldn't go to another party unless it was Adam's wedding and not much chance of that, right?

The band started playing 'Kalijah.' The fiddles screamed louder and faster and all the Juckets looked around expectantly but Elgin stayed in his seat. Finally, as the music grew to a crescendo, young Artie the-one-man-party got up on the table. He bowed towards Elgin, raised his hands, and at the final notes, he dove down onto his head.

The tradition continues.

—The End—